ROAD to LONDON

Other books by Barbara Mitchelhill

Storm Runners
Dangerous Diamonds
Run Rabbit Run

For younger readers
The Damian Drooth Supersleuth series:

The Case of the Disappearing Daughter
The Case of the Pop Star's Wedding
How to be a Detective
Spycatcher
Serious Graffiti
Dog Snatchers
Under Cover
Gruesome Ghosts
Football Forgery

ROAD to LONDON

BARBARA MITCHELHILL

ANDERSEN PRESS
LONDON

First published in 2012 by
Andersen Press Limited
20 Vauxhall Bridge Road
London SW1V 2SA
www.andersenpress.co.uk

British Library Cataloguing in Publication Data available.

ISBN 978 1 84939 407 9

Printed and bound by CPI Group (UK) Ltd, Croydon, CR0 4YY

For Helen

Stratford-upon-Avon

Chapter 1

A Strange Meeting

One summer's day when I was thirteen, something amazing happened. For months I had dreamed of a new life far away from Stratford. An actor's life. An exciting life filled with fame and fortune. And that afternoon, that summer's day, was when it all began.

It was hot, I remember. I was sitting in the school room with fifty sweating boys, pretending to study. Flies buzzed around my head. Sweat dripped off the end of my nose and onto my Latin text while my eyes grew heavy and began to close.

'Thomas Munmore! You are sleeping!'

The master's voice boomed across the school room and his birching stick cracked like a pistol shot as he struck his desk. My eyes snapped open and I sat bolt upright, waiting for him to march over and give me a beating. But in the sweltering heat the master had no energy for a flogging. Instead he lolled in his chair, red-faced and panting, with his blue robe drooping from his shoulders.

It had been a long and boring day for me, and when the church clock struck five I gladly stood up with all the other lads and bowed respectfully to our master. Then, as one, we tumbled down the stairs and out into the street, gasping for fresh air.

That day I didn't loiter. I had jobs to do before I could go down to the river and cool off. The sooner I started, the sooner I would be free to do as I pleased.

I raced across the town to Back Bridge Street where I had lived all my life in a crumbling old house with a poor thatch. There was one room downstairs where my sister, Beth, sewed and cooked, and Father mended shoes. Up above was our bedchamber, which was damp and bitterly cold in winter, and in summer filled with flies that landed on my face and crawled into my ears as I tried to sleep.

'Is the washing ready, Beth?' I called as I burst into the house. 'I want to go for a swim before the sun dies down.'

Father, who was working by the window, looked up from his bench, frowning. 'Swimming indeed,' he grumbled. 'Your sister has the linen ready, boy. You must take it at once.'

Beth tried to make up for Father's bad temper. 'The bed sheets are there, Thomas,' she said, smiling and nodding towards the basket on the table. 'They are to go to New Place. You know where that is, don't you?' she asked and winked at me.

Did I know where New Place was? Of course I did! Hadn't my hero – the famous Master William Shakespeare – bought the house two years ago? It was a fine house. One of the biggest in Stratford, with ten chimneys. Not that he lived in it. They said he only visited his family once or twice a year. Nowadays he was much too busy in London writing plays for the queen, and acting in the theatres.

I grabbed hold of the basket and rushed towards the door,

excited at the thought of visiting Master Shakespeare's house again.

'Go careful, boy,' Father snapped. 'No running or you'll tip it into the dirt.'

'And make sure you bring back the payment, Thomas,' Beth called after me – quite unnecessarily for I had delivered washing since I was six. I was well used to it.

Ignoring my father's instructions to go slowly I raced across town to New Place, thinking of my future as I carried the basket over my arm. One day I would be like Master Shakespeare. I'd go to London and act upon the stage. Soon my pockets would be full of gold, and I'd wear the best clothes and the finest boots and strut about the streets. One day.

By the time I turned into Chapel Lane the basket had grown so heavy that I was sweating unbearably and had to unbutton my doublet to cool myself. But finally I reached New Place. I pushed open the gate and walked into the garden where piles of wood and heaps of bricks had been left under trees by the path. The house had been in need of repair when Master Shakespeare bought it and after two years or more there were still masons and carpenters at work.

As I headed towards the door I caught sight of a man sitting in the shade of an oak tree. At first I thought he was a builder taking rest from his work, and although I didn't speak to him he must have heard my footsteps, for he turned round. Then, quite suddenly, he jumped to his feet and stared, making me stop in my tracks. I saw he was no workman, for his clothes were fine and well laundered.

And his trim beard and gold earring were sure signs of a wealthy man.

Seconds ticked by, my heart beating fast, as he fixed me with eyes so dark and piercing that I could neither move nor speak. Then I saw his hands begin to tremble, and he shook his head from side to side, groaning softly before uttering his first word, 'Hamnet.'

This meant nothing to me. I only knew I was afraid.

He spoke again, more quickly this time, his eyes wide and wild like a mad man's. He repeated the same word, over and over: 'Hamnet. Hamnet. Hamnet,' until he finally said, 'My son!' and stepped towards me, his arms stretched out to grasp me.

Terrified, I cried, 'Sir, I am not your son! I am Thomas Munmore. My sister has sent me with your linen.'

My words must have woken him from his trance for he blinked his eyes as if to clear his mind. His face turned so pale and ashen that I was afraid he would faint away.

'Sir,' I said again, reaching forward to take his elbow and stop him falling. 'You are unwell. Come and sit.' I led him back to the seat beneath the oak tree. There he rested, holding his head in his hands. I sat beside him waiting for him to calm himself. When he had, he turned and looked at me.

'Forgive me,' he said, placing his hand on mine. 'I was...I was shaken to see you there.' He pulled a handkerchief from his pocket and wiped his brow. 'You are the very image of my son, Hamnet, and I was certain I had seen his ghost.'

'His ghost?'

He nodded. 'Aye. He died of the plague two years ago, God save us. I was sitting here thinking of him when you came into the garden.' He stared at me with his dark, dark eyes. 'You are so like him, boy. He would have been your age now. About your height.' He sighed and shook his head. 'Heaven forgive me. I know I am blessed with two daughters. But Susanna and Judith can never replace my son.'

Daughters? Did he say his daughters were Susanna and Judith? Oh my stars! Instantly I recognised the names. I had met Susanna and Judith Shakespeare. They lived here, at New Place, with their mother. Judith was about my age and Susanna two years older. Now it was my turn to tremble as I realised that the man sitting next to me was their father, William Shakespeare. I could hardly contain my shock at being so close to the great man himself – the one I most admired in all the world. I stood up and stepped away as if I had no right to be sitting so near.

'Stay, Thomas,' he said, patting the seat next to him. 'Sit and talk to me. Tell me about yourself and how you see your future – for my own son has none.'

Nervously I settled back onto the seat.

'Tell me.' He repeated the words softly. 'How would you like your life to be?'

I swallowed and licked my lips so that I could speak. 'I would be an actor, sir.'

Master Shakespeare raised his eyebrows in surprise, then frowned a little. 'Nay, an actor's life is no life at all, wandering from town to town, not knowing where the next penny is to come from.'

'But – begging your pardon, sir – you are not a poor man.'

He smiled a slow, sad smile. 'I have been fortunate, Thomas. Most are not. Even my brother Edmund finds it hard to make a living on the stage.'

I got to my feet and stood in front of him to protest. 'But I wish to be like you, sir. I wish to go to London – to act and write plays. That is what I wish to do more than anything. I have acted in school plays – though they are in Latin and are very dull. But I believe I am the finest actor among all the boys. I promise you that I…'

Master Shakespeare smiled and lifted his hand to quieten me. 'I can see you are headstrong, Thomas. If that is your dream, nothing I can say will change it.' He paused, sitting and sighing a little before he said, 'My company of actors arrives in Stratford tomorrow to perform *A Midsummer Night's Dream* at the Guildhall. Have you seen the play, Thomas?'

I shook my head. 'We rarely have such entertainments in Stratford, sir. But I should like to go. I'm sure it will be a fine play.'

Then the great man stood up and walked to where I had left the basket on the ground. 'I thank you for the linen,' he said, taking a coin out of his purse and dropping it into my hand. 'Give this to your sister.'

I stared at the money. A shilling! 'But, sir, this is too much…'

'Not too much for hard work,' he insisted as he pulled another coin from his purse and gave it to me. 'This penny is for you, Thomas, to go and see the play. Perhaps you would like to meet the actors after the performance?'

I gasped at such an invitation. 'I shall be honoured, sir,' I replied and he smiled again, but I saw his eyes were wet with tears. Perhaps he was thinking of Hamnet, his poor dead son.

'Follow your dream, Thomas,' he said. 'Let it lead you where it may. I shall remember you, my boy. My blessings go with you.' He picked up the basket and walked away down the path towards the house.

Chapter 2

Exciting News

I ran out of the garden and into the street, eager to give Beth the money and tell her about my meeting with Master Shakespeare.

I was halfway along Chapel Lane, head down thinking about tomorrow's play, when a man stepped out of an alley and bumped into me, knocking me off balance and sending me crashing onto my back.

It was my cousin Richard.

'Whoa!' he laughed as I lay sprawled on the ground. 'Why such a hurry, Thomas?' Then he held out his hand and pulled me to my feet.

Richard was five years older than I and taller by a head. He had a crop of curly hair that was thick with sawdust for he was apprenticed to a joiner. Which is why there were two fingers missing from his left hand after a careless accident with a saw.

'I have news for you, coz,' he said as I stood there brushing the dirt off my doublet.

'What news?'

'Good news,' he replied and winked at me. 'Bessy Totthill saw your hero, Master Shakespeare, in the town this afternoon. "Oh," she says, "Master Shakespeare is so handsome, I almost swooned." Then she says, "Why can't you be like that,

Richard Munmore? Why can't you be rich and famous, eh?"'

Richard looked at me and roared with laughter. 'What cheek! I may not be famous but I'm handsome enough, aren't I, Thomas?'

He didn't need me to tell him he was handsome. Every wench in Stratford mooned over him, and Bessy Totthill would drag him to the church if she could.

'Well,' I said, 'I have news for you. I've just come from New Place and I met Master Shakespeare himself. I spoke with him, Richard. I sat by him in the garden and he talked to me.'

'Did he indeed?' Richard replied.

'He told me there was to be a play at the Guildhall tomorrow and he gave me a penny to go and see it.'

'What about your lessons?' Richard asked.

I laughed. 'I'll play truant! What does Latin grammar matter? I shall go and see the play, Richard. I will!'

A grin spread across his face, showing two crooked front teeth. 'Young devil, you are! Do as you please, coz, before you are saddled with a wife. Enjoy yourself while you are young.'

Then he took my arm and whispered in my ear. 'I'm off to Clopton's wood tonight. I'll fetch a rabbit for the pot, eh?'

I knew all about Richard's poaching. Father said he'd be caught one day but I knew he was too clever for the hangman's noose. He would always get away.

'I'll have fine sport.' he laughed. 'There's nothing that pleases me more than fooling Clopton's men.'

11

I usually liked to talk with Richard, but not today. I could only think about Master Shakespeare. What if we met again at the Guildhall? What if he invited me to join his players? I was thirteen and old enough to make my way in the world.

I hurried down the street, waving goodbye to Richard, and headed home, hardly able to contain my excitement.

Chapter 3
One Day

I arrived home to find my sister by herself still working at her sewing. Beth was older than me by three years and skinny as a lath but with kind brown eyes that anyone would trust. She had looked after my father, young John and me since our mother had been taken by the plague along with two other brothers. I was determined that, when I'd made my fortune in London, I'd buy a big house with servants to do the work and Beth would grow fat and lazy with good food. One day. Soon.

'I've got a surprise for you,' I said, jumping onto the edge of the table. 'Guess who I've just seen.'

Beth looked up as she rested her sewing on her lap and smiled.

'Go on! Guess!' I insisted.

She laughed and picked up her work again. 'I have been too busy to listen to gossip, Thomas,' she said, tucking a strand of fair hair under her mop cap. 'You'll have to tell me.'

'First you guess.'

'The queen,' she said, which was quite ridiculous.

'No, not the queen.'

'Then who?'

'Master Shakespeare!' I exclaimed. 'He's come to visit his family. I met him at New Place. He talked to me! And look how much he paid me for your washing.'

13

I put the shilling on the table and Beth's eyes grew wide. 'That is most kind of him,' she said, picking up the shilling and dropping it into the jar in the cupboard. 'Father will be glad, for he owes three weeks rent to Master Biddle.'

'One day, you won't have to worry about the rent for I shall be rich,' I told her and she laughed and settled back to her sewing.

'Master Shakespeare told me the most exciting news,' I said, hopping from one foot to the other. 'He's brought one of his plays to the Guildhall. It will be performed tomorrow and I will see it, Beth. I must.'

She held up her hand for me to stop. 'Thomas,' she said with a sigh as deep as a well. 'You have school tomorrow. How can you go to watch a play? You know you will not be allowed. The master frowns on such things.'

I sat on a stool next to her. 'It's only the afternoon. I expect the master will give me a flogging for it – but I've been beaten before. It's not so bad.'

I could see my sister was shocked. 'No, Thomas,' she insisted, her pale face grown serious. 'Father would be furious. No truanting. No play. And that's an end to it.' She pressed her lips tight together like Mother used to when she was angry. I reached across the table and tore a piece off the loaf for I was starving hungry. 'One day,' I said, chewing on the bread, 'I'll be a fine actor, just you wait and see.'

Beth sighed again and shook her head. She wouldn't hear any more and stabbed her needle into the cloth and went back to patching Mistress Biddle's old petticoat.

I was determined to keep her attention, so I leaped onto the table. 'Watch this, Beth!' I shouted, flinging my arms wide. 'See what you think of this.'

I had been practising my acting skills for months. The school plays were dull as ditch water. There was more to acting than walking around in togas spouting Latin. I would show my sister what I could do.

First, the ogre: I padded across the table, my back bent, my mouth hanging open, growling.

'I will steal you away,' I roared at her. 'And I will roast you in my oven!'

She raised an eyebrow, but said nothing.

Next I acted a chortling witch with long, scary fingers who cast spells. And, finally, I strutted like a king, holding my belly out in front like old King Henry.

'Sew me a fine silken shirt, wench,' I commanded, lifting my hand and pointing at Beth. 'And embroider it with gold or I shall chop off your head!'

Though I say it myself, it was a brilliant performance.

I stood there waiting for her applause but there was none – only the slightest twitch at the corner of her mouth as if she were trying not to laugh. So I jumped off the table and stood in front of her.

'One day, I shall go to London and become famous, Beth. I shall wear a gold earring and fine clothes and the best leather boots. And when I come back to Stratford, everybody will point and say, "There goes Master Munmore, the famous actor."'

My sister set down her sewing and sighed. 'One day! One

15

day! Don't talk such nonsense, Thomas. Actors are rogues. Master Shakespeare is not well liked in the town.'

'He gave you a shilling.'

'Aye, but does he look after his family as a man should? No. He stays away in London. Why do you worship him so, Thomas?'

'Because he is rich. He writes plays for the queen and they say he is a fine actor.'

'But his troupe of players are little more than vagabonds.'

'They are all fine men, I'm sure,' I laughed. 'No girl could live such a life.'

'Indeed, no!' she squealed, holding her hand over her mouth. 'It would be shameful for girls to strut upon a stage.'

'Shameful indeed. And it is against the law.'

Then she wagged her finger at me. 'But you are fortunate to have an education at the King's New School, brother. No such luck for me. While I grow old washing linen, you may find work in the church or the law or writing accounts.'

'No, Beth. I will not be a servant to anyone who cannot read nor spend my days writing wills. I want to be an actor,' I insisted. 'That's why I must see the play tomorrow.'

But she waved me aside. 'You will not disgrace us by playing the truant, Thomas. You must go to school. Say no more.' Turning away, she picked up her needle and continued her patching while I thought of the penny that Master Shakespeare had given me.

Chapter 4
A Plan Ruined

That night I hardly slept for thinking of the play. Lying between my father and my brother, John, I tossed about like a leaf in the wind, waiting for the sun to rise.

When the morning finally came and I returned to school, I couldn't concentrate on my Latin grammar. My mind wandered from my book as I turned the penny between my fingers, imagining what Master Shakespeare might say to me if I happened to see him at the play.

All morning my head was full of these thoughts as the church clock chimed away the hours. Seven...eight... nine...ten o'clock.

The school room was above the Guildhall where the play was to be performed. So, when I heard a cart rumble down Church Street and stop right outside, I guessed the troupe of players had arrived.

At last.

I heard them call to each other. 'Careful with those, Roger!' And then I heard a crash as something tumbled to the ground. 'Careful, I said! Don't damage the costumes.' My excitement increased.

I was listening to the activities outside when a shadow fell across the page of my book. I looked up and saw James Biddle, who was the son of Master Biddle our miserable landlord. This pinch-faced varlet was two years older than me and a monitor at school. He was just like his father – a tormentor and a bully who cared for no one but himself.

'Are you dreaming, Munmore?' he said in a clear voice so the master would hear. Then he suddenly bent over, his mouth close to my ear. 'I know that your father owes rent on your house,' he sneered in a low voice full of menace. 'He had better pay up or my father will throw you and your wretched family out into the street.'

I had no chance to reply before he snatched away my book and spoke again in a bold voice. 'On your feet, Munmore. Recite your Latin verse so I can see how well you have learned it.' He stood upright with the book open in his hands, knowing that the master was watching. He smirked, sure that I would fail and be rewarded with a beating.

But when I began to recite, his smile slipped from his face and soon changed to a frown. It was no surprise to me that I knew the page well. I had opened the book at a lesson I had learned days ago.

'How did I do?' I asked innocently.

James Biddle snorted, flung the book back on the table and stomped away to pester another lad.

At last the church clock chimed eleven and I hurried home to find Beth filling bowls with pottage.

My father had already left his workbench by the window. He had settled at the table, his back bent from too much work, his face wrinkled like an old man. Before my mother died, he hadn't looked so sad. I remembered that he often sang to us and made us laugh. But not now. Now he had the cares of the world on his shoulders. I sat on the bench next to him while Beth placed the bowls on the table. I spooned the pottage rapidly into my mouth. Tasteless as it was, it filled the grumbling hole in my stomach and I was grateful for it.

'Did you work well this morning, Thomas?' Father asked.

'I worked well, Father,' I said.

Beth was helping young John to the table. 'And did the master have anything to say about your writing?' she asked with a twinkle in her eye. 'Did he scold you for the ink blots on your paper?'

'No ink blots,' I replied, grinning at my sister.

My father finished his pottage and set his spoon in the dish. 'Are you sharpening your quills well?' he asked. 'Have you honed your penknife today?'

On my first day at the King's New School he had given me a present of a fine penknife and had carved my name upon it. An expensive gift from a poor cobbler. Since then he asked the same question every day for he was always anxious that I should take care of it.

'My penknife is sharp, Father. And my Latin is good and so is my writing. In fact,' I grinned, 'I am the perfect scholar.'

Beth laughed. 'And can a perfect scholar fetch me some water when he has finished his dinner?' she asked. 'The bucket is empty. I've been washing Mistress Biddle's linen all morning and I have spinning to do this afternoon.'

This was not good news. I needed to avoid the scholars returning for afternoon lessons, or they would see me heading for the Guildhall.

'Why do I have to fetch the water?' I complained.

Beth frowned. 'Then who will do it? Father has work to do and John is weak from the fever.'

John was younger than me by four years. He was a quiet lad and always sickly, it was true. As I looked at my poor brother's skinny frame, I thought that it might not be long before he joined our mother and brothers in the graveyard.

'But I must be back to school early,' I lied, 'or I will be in trouble.'

Beth glared at me. Did she suspect I was sneaking off to see Master Shakespeare's play?

'Do as your sister asks, Thomas,' Father said, his voice low and serious. 'You will also empty the bucket in the bedchamber. It is full to overflowing.'

I wanted to say no, but I didn't dare to argue for I would soon feel the flash of Father's anger if I did. I stood up from the table, quickly climbed the ladder to the bedchamber, returning more slowly with the bucket in my hand.

'Careful!' called Beth as she watched me descend. 'Don't let it slop over the edge.'

I walked towards the door carrying the putrid yellow liquid. No matter how often I did this job, the smell always made my stomach churn. I staggered outside, tipping the contents into the stinking watercourse which ran down the middle of the street. Father insisted that this was the right thing to do, but I wondered why we couldn't be like our neighbours who flung the piss out of the upstairs window.

Back inside, I returned the bucket to the bedchamber and picked up a pail to collect some water. I set off running towards the nearest well when a neighbour, seeing me with the bucket, called, 'Don't go to the well, Thomas. The heat has dried it out. Go to the river.'

I groaned inwardly and turned in the other direction. *Could anything else go wrong?* I wondered.

Well, yes, it could.

When I had reached the river, I hurried down to the water's edge and, in my haste to fill the bucket, slipped into the muddy bank. Now my shoes were covered with black slime, my stockings splashed.

By the time I had filled the pail and carried it back home I was sweating like a pig, and I looked like a vagabond. How could I go to the play looking like that? How could I hope that Master Shakespeare would speak to me? I found a rag and wiped myself down as best I could and smoothed my hair.

'How did you get into such a state, Thomas?' said Beth, laughing at my efforts to make myself tidy. 'Get off to school now or you'll be late.'

I didn't need to be told. I rushed out of the house and ran as fast as I could through the town, pulling my cap well down to hide my face. When I reached the high street the way was already crowded with people leaving their shops and homes to go to the Guildhall – such was the excitement at the arrival of the players. Stratford is a small town and there was little by way of entertainment. No wonder so many had come to watch.

The raucous throng, moved laughing and shouting up the street. Workmen, farmers, goodwives and maid servants. All were eager to see the play and so was I.

Six noisy apprentices, fresh from the ale house, were walking together, arms wrapped around each other's shoulders, shouting lewd jokes and guffawing. To keep myself out of sight of anyone who might know me I walked with the apprentices who didn't even notice me for I was so much smaller than them. Bubbling with excitement, we bumped and jostled along the road. No learning Latin grammar for me that afternoon. Instead I would be watching *A Midsummer Night's Dream* written by the best playwright in the whole country.

As we turned into Chapel Street the crowd slowed down and formed a queue that shuffled slowly into the Guildhall. I was almost there and I gave a sigh of relief that I had not been spotted – until fingers dug into my arm and a voice said, 'Do you play the truant this afternoon, Munmore?'

I turned and looked up into the flinty eyes of James Biddle.

'A scholar has no time for watching travelling players,' he sneered.

I tried to wriggle out of his grasp, hoping the apprentices would come to my aid. But they did not. They thought it was a great joke that I had been spotted and would be hauled back to my lessons. They laughed as Biddle tightened his grip.

'Come with me, Munmore,' the bully said and twisted my arm behind my back so that I cried out with the pain of it and thought it would surely snap in two.

Then he dragged me along the street and pulled me up the stairs into the school room.

The master stood and watched as we scuttled to our benches, ready for afternoon lessons. All the boys were frightened of him for he had a fearful temper and held a birch rod to remind us what would happen if we misbehaved. Not that we needed reminding. Every day someone got a beating for talking in class or fighting or coming in late or anything that the master fancied.

Today his frown was deeper than usual and his lips were pressed tight together as if he had the belly ache. We sat in silence, our eyes fixed on him, waiting for him to speak.

When he did, his voice was low and grave. 'This afternoon,' he growled, 'the town is in uproar because a troupe of players has arrived.' He leaned forward, one hand flat on his desk, and glared with eyes as black as the devil. 'You must not let the noise of all this disgraceful merry-making distract you. Do you hear? You must not!'

Then he raised the birch rod above his head and brought it smashing onto a table with a *CRACK!*. He intended this as a warning. But something happened that he had not intended. A large bottle of ink was sent rolling off the edge and crashing to the floor. There was an audible gasp in the classroom and all eyes were on the thick black liquid as it spread across the floorboards and dripped through the gaps.

'Biddle!' the master roared. 'See to it!' And he turned his back on the black puddle and walked away as if the accident had never happened.

James Biddle's eyes roamed around the room, looking for a suitable boy to clear up the mess. And when they rested on me, he pointed and said, 'Munmore! Mop up the ink and go and mix some more.'

'But...'

'Do you argue?' he sneered.

I said nothing but went to fetch a cloth and kneeled down to wipe up the spilled ink. It was a dirty job, staining my hands and fingernails and splashing my sleeves. Had I ever looked in a more sorry state? I picked the bottle off the floor and left the room to go and make more ink, boiling with anger that Biddle had ruined my chance of seeing the play.

I walked down the corridor towards a large cupboard where the ingredients for the ink were stored and, as I did, I heard a roar of laughter from the crowd in the street. The window was too high to see out of but I stood on a bench and looked down to the street below. One of the players – a stout, comic fellow – was jesting with the crowd to keep them entertained while they waited to go into the Guildhall. The sight of them making merry made me feel more miserable than ever. I should have been with them.

I watched for a while before stepping off the bench and going to make the ink. It was a messy business mixing sticky gum Arabic, green vitriol and galls. I'd done it many times. I opened the door to the cupboard and set the ink bottle on the shelf. But I couldn't help asking myself – did I want to mix ink? Or did I want to see the play? And did I care if I got a beating tomorrow?

I looked down at my hands already stained black from mopping the floor. *No more of this!* I thought. *Follow your dream, Thomas Munmore! Go!* And I ran down the stairs and out into the street.

Chapter 5
A Forest of Legs

Keeping an eye open for any neighbour who might recognise me, I again joined the queue for the play as it jostled through the gate and under the archway that led to the Guildhall.

'Will we all get in?' the woman in front of me asked her husband. 'There are so many of us.'

Indeed the crowd was squeezed into the tunnel-like entrance, edging forward until we burst out like cannon balls into the courtyard where a boy was sitting at a small table taking money. He was about fifteen – a real bag of bones with long greasy hair dangling over his spotty face. The shirt he wore was two sizes too big and I suspected it had once been white.

'Where's your penny, then?' he said, chewing on a straw. I pulled the coin from my doublet and placed it in his outstretched hand.

'Why ain't you at school, shrimp?' he asked, dropping the penny into a box. 'Playing truant, are you?'

I shook my head.

'Don't believe you. Look at you with your doublet and hose. That's a scholar's garb, that is.'

'I'm apprentice to a shoemaker,' I lied. 'My master has let me come to see the play.'

Before he could ask more questions, I walked past the table

and pushed my way into the Guildhall, which was already full to bursting and filled with the noisy chatter of town's folk. Although I had managed to get inside, I was stuck at the back with my view blocked by tall men and their buxom wives. If I was to see the stage I needed to get to the front. But how? I tried pushing. I tried wriggling. It was no good. I could not find a way through the audience because they were jammed together like logs in a wood store.

There was only one thing to do.

I dropped onto my hands and knees and began to crawl through the forest of legs. This was not easy, and more than once heavy boots stepped on my hands and I feared I might lose my fingers. But I carried on, pushing on ankles and squeezing through legs which caused all sorts of grunts and yowls.

At last I emerged from under the petticoats of a jolly lady in the front row.

'*Oooooh*, my word! What creature have we here?' she squealed, clapping her hands to her cheeks.

'I'm Thomas, madam,' I replied from my kneeling position. And when she looked down and saw me, she clutched her generous stomach and rocked with laughter.

'Well, Thomas,' she said, taking my hand and helping me up, 'you stand next to me, my lovely. It will be a fine play, I'm sure, for it is one of Master Shakespeare's. *A Midsummer Night's Dream* it's called, and they say it is mighty amusing.'

An old man standing next to her leaned forward. 'Will Kemp is to play a part.'

'Is he famous?'

'Aye, lad. The finest comic in the land. I reckon that he's more famous than Master Shakespeare.'

I didn't believe that. No one could be more famous. That was impossible.

'Will Master Shakespeare take a part?' I asked.

'That I don't know,' said the old man, shaking his head. 'But, if not, he might come and watch to make sure the play goes well.'

Master Shakespeare's house was just a few paces from the Guildhall. He would surely come. He must come. I felt faint at the thought of speaking to him again. But I snapped out of my imaginings when a player dressed in green stepped onto the stage and walked about banging a drum till the crowd quietened, ready for the performance to begin.

I must admit, I didn't like the play at first. It was all about love which isn't very interesting. And there were fairies in it too, and they didn't look a bit like fairies.

But the next part of the play was very funny. A group of workmen came strutting onto the stage, rehearsing a play for the Duke Theseus. Will Kemp played Bottom, the most stupid and the funniest of all the workmen who was turned into an ass and could only make *hee-haw* noises. He was brilliant. I laughed till tears poured down my face and my stomach ached.

'I told you he was a fine comic,' said the woman next to me, and I nodded in agreement as I wiped my cheeks on my shirt sleeve.

Everyone enjoyed the play and we cheered and clapped until our hands were sore. Just when I thought it had ended,

Will Kemp jumped up and began a fine old jig. He was powerfully built with a grizzled beard and long hair and had amazing energy for a man of middling years. He bounced and jumped and tumbled – making the crowd shriek with laughter until he announced that the play was done and we were to go home.

'That was marvellous, was it not, Thomas?' the jolly lady asked as we turned to leave the Guildhall.

I nodded. 'The best thing I ever saw,' I said. 'But where is Master Shakespeare?'

'I expect he's backstage with the actors, my lovely,' she said. 'He's a busy man.'

I stood quite still, buzzing with the excitement of that afternoon. I had dared to run away from school. I had dared to watch the play. And I would not go home yet for Master Shakespeare had asked if I would like to meet the actors. This was my lucky day, I could feel it.

While the crowd filed out into Chapel Street, I hid in the recess of a door in case anyone might spot me and tell my father. I waited until the audience had gone and soon after that the actors appeared. They had already changed into their everyday clothes and began packing costumes into boxes – silk dresses dotted with pearls, velvet breeches and coloured hose. They must have been worth a king's ransom.

I watched them for a while and, to tell the truth, as I stood in the shadow my confidence began to drain away. Dare I speak to these fine actors? I was just a boy. I would only make a fool of myself, I thought.

When the church clock struck five I realised that if I didn't act now, they would soon be gone, moving on to the next town.

Do it, Thomas Munmore, I said to myself. Then, before I could change my mind, I stepped out of my hiding place.

Chapter 6

An Invitation

I wondered who I should speak to. All the actors were now busy carrying the boxes and props and loading them onto a cart waiting in the street. I recognised some of the boys, who had played the parts of love-sick girls and fairies. I was thinking I might talk to them when Master Kemp walked in with the thin boy who had collected the money. The comic seemed like a friendly man and I thought he might help me. I took my courage in both hands and walked towards him.

It seemed that everybody saw me approaching. The actors looked across at me. The boys pointed and laughed so that I suddenly felt embarrassed and stood stock-still with a gormless expression on my face.

'What's with you, lad?' called Master Kemp. 'Are you a stage-struck loon wanting to join our troupe?'

'We get plenty of those,' laughed the skinny lad by his side.

His words wounded me like a knife, but I stepped nearer. 'No, sir, I am not,' I said, bold as you like. I frantically searched inside my brain for a good reason to be there and said, 'I saw the play and I have a suggestion for you.'

'What suggestion?'

'For the ass, sir.'

'What about the ass?'

'I think it would be better if you used pieces of leather for its ears. Then they wouldn't flop. I know about leather as my father is a cobbler.'

Will Kemp stroked his grizzled beard. 'Well, well,' he said. 'An excellent idea. Smart boy.'

'I am, sir.'

'Indeed!'

'And I wish to become an actor when I am older.'

He laughed and slapped his knees. 'Ah, I was right. You are stage struck!' He put his hand on my shoulder. 'Then tell me what you thought of the play.'

My heart pounded against my chest as I tried to speak.

'It was a good play, sir, but...' The words dried in my mouth.

I looked at Will Kemp hoping this would be enough. He looked at me and smiled.

'But...?' he said, raising his eyebrows.

I took a deep breath and tried again to say something that would make sense. 'All those Italian names, sir.'

'Yes? What of the names?'

'Well they are hard for ordinary folk to understand and I think the plot is too complicated.'

Will Kemp took his hand off my shoulder. He was still looking at me but he was no longer smiling. 'How do you mean "complicated"?'

'Well...er...it needs to be simpler,' I said.

Now Master Kemp was frowning.

'There was too much love in it,' I blurted out, then stood, holding my breath, waiting for his reaction.

32

Master Kemp's eyes did not leave me. Was he angry that I had criticised Master Shakespeare's play? At that moment, I felt sick. I should have held my tongue. I wished I had said nothing at all.

But suddenly Master Kemp threw back his head and laughed. 'Too much love! Well, well, well!' he said, slapping me on the shoulder. ''Tis a pity that Will Shakespeare is not here. That would have amused him. But he is doing business with the town council.'

I was pleased that I had made him laugh and I grabbed the opportunity to say what I really wanted to. 'Sir, I would like to act and write plays like Master Shakespeare. I am a scholar and can read and speak lines well.'

Master Kemp looked at me seriously. 'Can you indeed? And why do you wish to be an actor, boy? Do you think you will be rich?'

I shrugged.

'Look at us all,' he said, pointing at the players loading the cart. 'Do we look rich?'

They did not. Their clothes were coarse and dirty and even more worn than my own.

'But you have come from London and London is a grand place,' I insisted, for at that time I believed the streets of the city were paved with gold.

Master Kemp shook his head. ''Tis no life for you, my lad,' he said. 'When there is an outbreak of the plague, the queen keeps the playhouses closed for fear of spreading it. We have been forced to travel the countryside these last two

33

months to earn our keep – little more than vagabonds.'

'But you are here in the Guildhall.'

'Aye. Because Master Shakespeare persuaded the town councillors to grant us a licence. In most places we are as beggars performing at any inn that will have us.' Master Kemp suddenly smiled as if to brush away the gloom. 'But today we shall leave Stratford and return to our playhouse in London.'

'Can I come with you?'

'Work at your studies, boy, and you will earn more than any actor.' With that he turned and walked off, but I followed and stood in front of him to block his way.

'I don't want to study and become a lawyer in the courts. I want to act and write,' I insisted.

He paused for a moment, resting his hand on my shoulder. 'Then when you are older, if you still feel the same, come to London and seek us out. Our troupe is called the Lord Chamberlain's Men, and William Shakespeare is one of us.'

He left me feeling stunned, my head filled with his words: *'Come to London and seek us out.'* As I stepped into the street, I went over them in my mind…over and over…He had invited me to join his troupe of actors when I was older. But how old was that? How long would I have to wait before I could go?

When I reached home Beth was standing at the grate, stirring the pot ready for our supper. She glanced over her shoulder and, unsmiling, nodded towards Father who was at his bench mending some boots.

'Father wishes to speak with you, Thomas,' she said quietly.

Those words did not bode well. I went and stood by him until he looked up from his work and I saw that his eyes flashed with anger. He lay down his tools and spoke in his low voice which always filled me with dread.

'You disgrace me, Thomas,' he growled. 'You missed your afternoon lessons and instead you went to a play.' He spat out the word 'play' as if it was poison and I hung my head. 'Where did the money come from for such a thing? Did you steal it, boy?'

'No. I was given a penny by…'

'So you do not deny going to the Guildhall?'

There was no point in denying it. Someone must have seen me and come running to tell him. I said nothing more, but stood there waiting, shaking with fear.

'Have you no shame?' Now his voice roared and my knees began to knock. 'You were taken into the King's New School because you have a fine brain.' Father stood up from the bench and began to unbuckle his belt. 'I will not see you waste your education. I will not! Now take down your breeches.'

I won't describe the thrashing I got. One thrashing is much like another and it left my backside raw and sore. All that night I lay downstairs with neither supper nor drink nor a mattress to sleep on. But no amount of pain could stop me thinking of Master Kemp's invitation. That night, when I fell asleep, I dreamed a long and happy dream of travelling the road to London.

Chapter 7
A Painful Outcome

When Beth came down the next morning I was still asleep. 'It is gone half-past five, Thomas,' she said. 'Get yourself off to school. Father's mood is no better today so you should leave quickly before he comes down.'

I struggled to my feet and felt my breeches sticking to my backside with dried blood; I eased them away as best I could. That done, I dipped my hands in the water bucket to wash the ink from them and splashed my face to clean off yesterday's grime. I was stiff as a board from the beating and from sleeping on the floor, while my stomach rumbled for want of food. Breakfast was almost two hours away – if the master allowed me any. No doubt he would also punish me severely for playing truant.

The thought of another beating made me turn to Father's workbench, where I found a piece of leather large enough to cover my backside. I quickly stuffed it under my breeches knowing it would soften the blow of the master's birch rod.

Trying not to think about the beating I hurried out of the house and ran up the street, heading towards school. As I turned into the high street I saw a group of classmates walking together. I waved and shouted, expecting them to call back to me. Usually they would say, 'Ho, Thomas! Are you swimming in the river after school?' Or, 'Come and kick a ball with us.' But that day they said nothing. Some looked away. Some stared at me. Some even smirked. They all knew I was in serious trouble and knew what was going to happen. The master would be there when we arrived, trembling with fury at what I had done. His flogging would come next and that would be a terrible thing.

As we climbed the stairs no one spoke. There was only the sound of boys' footsteps reluctantly making their way to the school room. As we entered the usher was waiting for us as usual and we doffed our caps to show respect. Finally the master swept in, his gown flowing behind him like an enormous, terrifying bat. We kneeled and clasped our hands together while he recited a prayer in Latin and I prayed for strength.

Then we stood and James Biddle called out our names from the register before checking our hands and faces. That morning two of the smallest boys were sent outside to wash again.

We sat down. I lowered my sore backside onto the bench and waited for what was to come. Everyone's attention was on the master standing at the front.

At first he did not speak. Instead, he paced backwards and forward, slapping his birch rod onto the palm of his hand and glowering under his cap in my direction. My whole body was trembling with fear. I could not help it. Then the master roared, 'Munmore! Stand!' and cracked the birch twigs on the edge of the table so that my heart leaped into my mouth.

I pulled myself up but was shaking so badly that my legs could barely support me. I leaned against the table to stop myself falling and I tried to hold my chin high so I would not look afraid.

The master glared at me with gimlet eyes set deep in hollow sockets. 'You have some explaining to do,' he growled. 'Come forward.'

As steadily as I could I walked to the front and stood before him while he listed my crimes from the day before. He went on and on. About the ink. About my truanting. About my watching a shameful play. A scholar does not do this, he said. A scholar does not do that.

Finally, he ran his fingers along the full length of the birch rod and an evil smile spread across his face. 'Bend over, Munmore,' he said, relishing the thought of the flogging, while I broke out into such a sweat that I can scarcely remember leaning over the bench.

But I do remember that it was James Biddle who stepped forward to hold me down and, as he did so, he whispered in my ear, 'One day I'll have my turn, you little turd-weavil.'

His leering face was the last thing I saw before the pain of the first stroke shot through me. After that, I squeezed my eyes shut and gritted my teeth.

One lash. Two. Three lashes. Four.

On and on it went and with every stroke I thought of London...London...London.

Chapter 8
A New Plan and a Pigeon

When school was finished for the day my backside was raw and agonizingly painful. I was angry and in no mood to go home. Instead, I went to seek out my cousin Richard and found him leaving the house off Chapel Lane where he was working.

'I need your help,' I said.

'I need some ale,' he replied, brushing the wood shavings from his hair. 'I've been mending floorboards in Master Sydney's bedchamber all day and my mouth is dry as dust.' He tossed his bag of tools over his shoulder and set off down the street.

'Listen!' I said, running beside him. 'I need money.'

'Why so?'

'Because I am going to London.'

'Are you indeed? Do you plan to leave your schooling behind?'

'I am finished with schooling. I am determined to go to London but I need money to get there.'

'I have none to lend, coz,' Richard replied and winked at me. 'How can I court Bessy Totthill if I lend my money to you?'

'I am not asking you to.'

'What then?'

'I want you to take me poaching so I can earn money. Sell rabbits or fish or whatever I catch.'

Richard stopped and looked down at me. 'No, Thomas. Going to London is one thing but poaching...' He walked on, placing his hand on my shoulder. 'It's a treacherous business and you are only a boy.'

I pushed his hand off in irritation. 'I am not a child,' I snapped. 'I am sick of school. I am sick of beatings. I'm old enough to make my way in the world.'

'In London?'

'Aye.'

'What about your father? What about Beth? Do they know of this?'

'No. They'd only try to stop me. But they'll be better off with one less mouth to feed. And when I make my fortune I'll send money home.' I gave him all the reasons for leaving Stratford, but it didn't make any difference. Richard wasn't listening.

I tugged at his shirt sleeve in one last attempt. 'Take me poaching. Please!' I begged.

But my cousin shook his head. 'If you were caught it would mean prison and a hand chopped off. Even hanging.'

'I won't get caught,' I insisted. 'You poach on Clopton's land often enough and you don't get caught. I'll do anything you say. But I need money for I must leave soon.'

'Why so urgent, coz?'

'Because I mean to be an actor with Master Shakespeare. Will Kemp himself invited me to join the Lord Chamberlain's Men.' This was not exactly true but it suited my purpose.

40

Richard laughed. 'If you must be an actor, coz, then go when you are older.'

'No. I need to get away, Richard. I must go soon.'

He laughed and punched me on the shoulder. 'But I will not take you poaching,' he said. 'It is too dangerous.' Then he waved his hand and, without another word, he walked off.

I could not let it rest. My head was filled with the thought of going to London and, if Richard wouldn't help me, there was only one thing to do. I would go poaching on Clopton's land by myself.

Thomas Clopton was a wealthy man who lived on the far side of town at Clopton Hall; a huge, rambling house with six or seven chimneys and a great deal of land around it with stabling for ten horses. Master Clopton rode with hounds across his fields to keep foxes at bay and there was gossip in the town that he was a heavy drinker and a cruel master. For both these reasons I knew it was dangerous, but I was desperate. I had to go.

My plan was to take fish from the large pond close to the hall. I'd heard that it was kept well stocked with pike and perch. I knew how to fish. I was good at it. I didn't need Richard to teach me that.

'The sooner I do it,' I said to myself, 'the sooner I'll have money enough to leave.'

I kept some string and a hook in my doublet for I often went fishing for tiddlers in the river. All I needed was some bait and I kept a secret store down by the Avon. Some days ago I had hidden a dead pigeon behind a wall where no one would see it. By now the rotting bird would be full of juicy maggots and perfect for the fish. I ran to the river, found the pigeon and pushed its rigid body inside my doublet.

Tingling with excitement, I set off through the town and headed towards Clopton's land.

The whole of the estate was bounded by thick blackthorn hedges to keep strangers off his fields and out of his woods. But I found a small gap and managed to push my way through, not caring that my hands were scratched and my shirt was torn. What matters a shirt? When I had made my fortune in London I would have a dozen shirts.

On the other side of the hedge a hill sloped down to Clopton Hall. The top of the hill was thick with oak trees and beeches and hazel saplings. I crouched under the canopy of leaves keeping out of sight while I pulled the string and hook from my doublet. Then, taking my penknife, I cut a twig of hazel for a fishing rod and tied the string to it. I was ready.

Between the wood and Clopton Hall was a large stretch of meadow. I knew that once I left the cover of the trees I might be seen. My heart was already racing at the thought of it. I squatted at the edge of the wood, looking down at the fish pond and seeking out any movement around the hall or in the yard. But there was no one about. Not even a stable lad. It was time to go.

I raced over the fields at top speed, keeping low – knees bent and head down – always on the lookout for Clopton's men. When I came to the fish pond I flung myself into the reed beds which surrounded it and lay there panting, relieved to be out of sight. But Clopton's hounds, on the other side of the stables, must have heard me for they started barking and howling. I was terrified. Somebody was sure to go and see what the cause of all the noise was. I waited. No one came and eventually the hounds went quiet and I felt safe again, hidden among the reeds.

Slowly, I sat up and squatted by the pond's edge. I slipped my hand into my doublet and pulled out the rotting pigeon. With my penknife I slit open its belly and picked two of the fattest maggots and fixed them squirming onto the end of the line. Then I pushed the rod through the reeds and over the pond, letting the bait drop silently into the water.

For some time nothing happened, but just as I was thinking that my first attempt at poaching would come to nought, I felt a jolt on the line. I gripped the rod and pulled. But I couldn't pull hard enough. I needed to stand up. I struggled to my feet and dug my heels into the soft ground on the edge of the water. Then, squeezing my fingers tight around the rod, I leaned back and tugged with all my strength until, suddenly, a huge pike came flying out of the pond, spraying me with water and thrashing violently on the end of the line. Its mouth was open, its vicious teeth were clearly visible and I staggered backwards, arms flailing, and landed in the muddy ground of the reed bed. As for the pike, it flopped beside me twitching, grey and glistening and gasping for breath until I grabbed a stone and stunned it into stillness.

I sat back, amazed at my luck, thinking how much money

the pike would fetch. Maybe I would only need one more and I would have enough money to set out on my journey.

When I came to my senses, I realised that the hounds were barking again and I heard voices. Angry voices. My stomach tightened and I began to tremble as I parted the reeds and looked through. Three men, tall and wide-shouldered in the way of men who work the land, were running from the stables. One was wielding a stout stick while another brandished a pitch fork.

'Poacher!' shouted one, pointing in the direction of the pond. 'Adam, go back and let out the hounds.'

I knew I had to go but panic overtook me. My legs almost gave way as I tried to stand. I knew I must run. If I didn't, they would catch me and I would be done for.

Chapter 9
A Knock at the Door

I flung the rod into the reeds and grabbed hold of the pike. But, as I scrambled to my feet, the fish slithered through my fingers and fell to the ground. There was no time to pick it up. I couldn't. I had to run for my life.

Across the field I kept low, hoping that the men wouldn't see me. I raced over the grass and up the hill, back into the wood. I could hear them not far behind but I was gasping and my lungs were almost bursting with the effort.

I stopped at a fork in the path, resting my hands on my knees to catch my breath. Which way to turn? Left or right? There was no time to hesitate. I set off down a narrow track and, just as I was putting distance between me and the men, my foot caught in a mesh of brambles. I flung out my arms to try to save myself, but down I went, propelled headlong into the thorny tangle where I lay wheezing for lack of air.

I did not hear the panting of dogs but I did hear men's footsteps. They were closer. Not far off now. So I did the only thing I could. I dragged myself away from the path and lay, scratched and bleeding, but well hidden under a low bush. Nearer and nearer the men came and I hardly dared to breathe as they paced this way and that and strode around in circles as if they knew I must be somewhere close.

'He's here. He has to be!' one man shouted to the other. 'Keep looking. The varmint's likely hiding in the undergrowth.'

Then I heard, 'Over here, Jack,' and they began beating at the brambles with their sticks.

I stuffed my hand into my mouth, afraid that if they struck at the bush where I was hiding I might shout out and they would find me. To my relief, I heard them turn away and their footsteps fade as they began to search in another direction.

This was my chance. I wriggled forward, keeping my belly on the ground and pushing with my knees. When I was well away from the men, I scrambled to my feet and ran as if the Devil himself was after me.

I thought I had escaped but I had not. The noise of baying hounds spread across the fields. They were excited to be free and on the chase, sent to sniff me out like a fox in its lair. They would find me and tear me to pieces as Master Clopton had trained them to do.

Wild with fear I ran, not knowing where I was going. The twisted branches of the trees waved above me, dark and menacing, their roots forming tangled knots, ready to trip me. Tree trunks were all around, closing in and trapping me in the wood.

I did not know which way to run, but my legs must have known, for they took me in the right direction. Before the hounds could sniff me out, the hedge appeared in front of me and the road to Stratford was on the other side. I could see no gap to squeeze through so, in desperation, I flung myself at it, grabbing hold of the thorny branches. Somehow, I managed to scramble over the top and drop down on the other side. I was free.

It was not an easy walk home. I was exhausted, bruised and bleeding from the scratches. When I reached our house, Beth was alone mending Father's shirt by the light of the candle. John was already in bed and Father was away at the Angel.

Beth looked up, resting her sewing on her lap. 'Thomas!' she said, shocked at my appearance. 'Have you been in a fight?'

'Just larking about,' I lied.

'And were you larking about by the river?' she asked, pointing to my shoes and stockings which were wet from the fish pool. 'Don't let Father see you. Off to bed before he gets back from the tavern.'

I lit a candle and climbed up to the chamber where John lay coughing in his sleep. I dropped my shoes by the bed and peeled off my wet hose and draped them over the chair. It was only when I unbuttoned my doublet and pulled out the remains of the pigeon that I noticed my penknife was missing. I searched the room, thinking I had just dropped it, but it wasn't there. Had I left it in the school room? I remembered I'd used it that afternoon to sharpen my quill. I climbed into bed next to John who groaned and wriggled and coughed but did not wake, and I blew out the candle.

But I couldn't sleep with so many things buzzing round in my head. I was lying there, wondering how much the pike would have fetched at market when, suddenly, I heard a loud knocking at the door. 'Mistress Munmore?' someone asked as Beth opened it.

'Indeed I am,' she replied.

'I am Master Clopton's man and I would speak with you.'

I leaped out of bed, pressed my eye to the gap in the floor-board and saw a stout, red-faced man push his way past Beth and enter our house.

'A lad was seen poaching on our land,' he said, 'and I believe he lives here.'

Beth looked pale and very anxious. 'Why so?' she asked.

'This was found by the fish pond alongside a dead pike,' he said, reaching into his doublet.

I was done for. He was holding my penknife in his hand, my name carved clearly on the handle.

'Does Thomas Munmore live here?'

Beth hesitated and I kneeled there, terrified, waiting for her to reply.

'He is my brother,' she said.

'And is he at home?'

She didn't speak.

Clopton's man gripped her arm. 'It will be the worse for you if you do not say.'

'Let me go!' she protested. 'You will find him at the Angel. I sent him there to fetch our father.'

'Very well,' the man said as he turned to go. 'I shall seek him out and take him before the justice. Good day to you, mistress.' Then he marched from the house, slamming the door behind him.

He had hardly gone before I was fully dressed and hurtling down the ladder.

'I am done for, Beth. What shall I do?'

She took me by the shoulders and shook me. 'Have you been poaching, Thomas? Tell me the truth.'

'H-help me, Beth!' I stammered. 'Help me!'

She held up her hands in a gesture of despair. 'What on earth possessed you?' she asked. 'Punishments are bad enough for trespassing on another man's land – poaching is far worse. What happened to those brains of yours, Thomas?'

'But what shall I do?' I repeated.

'Get away from here. If you stay you will go before the justice of the peace and your life will be over.'

My stomach, already knotted with fear, began to tremble and I gasped for air until I thought that I should faint. Visions of prison cells and the hangman's noose danced before my eyes. Richard had been right. Poaching was a dangerous game, and I had just lost.

But Beth, practical as ever, was already wrapping some bread and cheese in a cloth. 'Take this,' she said, handing me the parcel. 'Go now. Leave Stratford, but stay away from the towns and villages for you have no licence to travel and you'll be sent back if you are found. Look for a farm, Thomas. Get work as quick as you can and send us word that you are safe.'

I opened the door and as I did, Beth called, 'Wait,' and turned to pick the jar from the cupboard and empty some of the coins into her hand. 'Take this,' she gave the money to me. 'Use it wisely – only when you need to.'

With that, she kissed my forehead and we said goodbye.

The Road to London

Chapter 10
A Meeting in a Wood

I ran from my home and through the streets, sneaking along alleyways and keeping close to the walls. I was soon at the Avon, which was low after the hot summer, and I slipped down to the water's edge to stay hidden from view. I took off my shoes and waded along the river until I reached the bridge, which carried the road south out of Stratford, and I climbed onto it. With hard ground beneath my feet I was able to move more quickly. On and on I ran until I had no breath and had to slow to a walk, hoping that Clopton's men were far behind me or, better still, had now given up the chase.

By then the light had faded, but there were no clouds to block out the moon that night and so I could see quite clearly. With no moon I would have had to travel in complete darkness, and who knows what trouble I might have stumbled into. There were cut-throats and thieves on the roads, looking for easy prey, and they would not hesitate to pounce. And if a traveller had no money, they might pull out his teeth or cut off his hair to sell. This was no night to be carefree, believe me.

When I was well away from Stratford I walked steadily, planning what I should do. Beth had told me to find work on a farm but ploughing fields and pulling turnips wasn't the life I wanted. If I followed this road I would reach London – that was certain – and eventually I might find Master Shakespeare.

What did it matter if it took me four days or fourteen? I'd manage on what food I had and I'd get there in the end. Somehow.

I walked on until my heels were rubbed as raw as liver and my legs cried out for rest. On one side of the road was a wood thick with trees and gorse and brambles where I would be well hidden from robbers.

I left the highway and stumbled into the wood, pushing back branches that barred my way, until I came to a clearing where I found an old oak tree that had been struck by lightning. Its trunk was split almost in two, making a perfect place to sleep. Too tired to eat, I climbed inside and lay back on the soft moss that grew on the bark. My eyes grew heavy and my lids drooped, but when I heard an animal howl some way off I trembled, afraid that it might be a wolf. But even this thought could not keep me awake for long and I fell into a deep sleep.

The next morning I woke early to find myself shaking with cold. The hot summer had suddenly been replaced by a bitter autumn wind. Even though I wrapped my arms around my chest and pulled my doublet tight, I could not escape the chill. Then, as I clambered out of the tree trunk, I felt the first spots of rain.

I went to shelter under an ash tree as the rain fell steadily, and I opened Beth's parcel of bread and cheese. I was about to take my first bite when I heard a noise in the clearing behind me – twigs cracked underfoot and there was heavy breathing and an odd snorting.

I spun round and almost cried out. A moment ago there had been no one there. Now there was a man of middle years, his face grey and unwashed with a straggly black beard hanging from his chin. He was dressed in a long black coat, torn and patched in many places. On his head he wore a battered hat and, in his right hand, I was surprised to see that he held the reins of a fine black horse.

'Well, well, well,' he said, swaggering towards me. 'A fellow traveller, I see.' Then he smiled, showing a mouth empty of teeth except for a few rotting, yellow stumps. His eyes, set deep under heavy black eyebrows, had something of the devil about them and I felt a chill of fear run through me.

'Some bread to share, lad?' he asked, as he tethered his horse to a tree.

Nervously, I tore off a piece and handed it to him.

He leaned against the trunk of the ash tree next to me and, as the rain beat on the canopy of leaves over our heads, he bit into the bread.

'So what's a young 'un like you doin' in the wood?' he asked, eyeing me as he chewed. 'Where's your parents, lad?'

I stuffed my mouth so full of bread that I could not reply.

'Have you run away from yer father, eh?' he chuckled. 'Did he give yer a beatin'?'

I finished chewing – though fear made it hard to swallow. 'I have no parents,' I lied. 'I'm travelling to London.'

At that, his eyes lit up and his mouth twitched into a smile of such evil intent that I stepped back two paces.

'Don't be nervous, lad,' he smirked. 'Naw! This is your lucky day. You can join me in a hadventure. Would you like that, eh?'

By then my shirt was soaked through. Water was dripping off my hair and rolling down my cheeks as the stranger placed his hands on my shoulders and leaned forward. Close up, I saw that his face was pitted with marks of the pox, and badly scarred. His breath was so vile and stinking that it turned my stomach.

'Did you hear me, lad?' he snarled and squeezed his fingers into my shoulders. 'I said, *Will you join me in an hadventure?*' When I didn't answer, his eyes narrowed and his eyebrows knitted together in a frown. 'Lost yer tongue, has yer?'

I shook my head.

'NO?' he shouted, suddenly lashing out and grabbing hold of my ear so that I screamed in pain. 'I just wants yer to do a nice little job for me, see.'

If I wanted him to stop, I knew I had to speak.

'W-what do I have to do?' I stammered.

'Easy,' he said, keeping hold of my ear. 'You just lies out on the road like you's had a haccident. When a gentleman comes along on his fine horse, he'll see you a-lying there and he'll stop and think, *Oh dear, here's a poor lad in trouble*. And he'll climb off his horse to come and help yer. And that's where I steps in.' He held out his index finger and drew it slowly across his neck. 'See?'

I stared at him. He was planning to kill and rob the next man to ride down this road. I felt sick at the thought of being a part of his plan. I couldn't do it. I shook my head frantically from side to side.

'You say no again?' the stranger roared and twisted my ear so viciously that it almost parted from my skull.

By then I was shaking from head to foot. This man terrified me more than anyone I had known. Not even the master's floggings or my father's belt or James Biddle's threat to cut out my tongue had scared me like this. My stomach was knotted with fear and I wrapped my arms about it to try and calm it down. But it churned and groaned. The bread and cheese were stirring and swelling inside my belly until it could hold them no longer. They rose up my throat and into my mouth and vomit erupted down the man's coat and all over his boots.

'Wretched, vile, disrespectful lad!' he yelled, flinging me to the ground into the pool of sick. Then he raised his foot and swung it at my backside which was still raw from the beatings. Again and again his great boot struck me until I was as limp as a puppet. I lay there powerless while he grabbed hold of my collar and dragged me towards the tree where the horse was tied. 'You'll help me if I say so,' he growled.

As he approached the animal it tossed its head and reared up, its forelegs pawing the air, its eyes wide and wild with terror.

'Down, yer brute,' he shouted and snatched a whip from inside his coat. Holding me in one hand, he raised the whip in his other. He held it above his head and brought it down on the horse's back again and again until its haunches were striped with blood. I shut my eyes, sickened by the sight. And when he had beaten the poor creature until it was too afraid to move, he reached for a rope hanging on the saddle and waved it in front of my face.

'You'll help me if I say so,' he repeated and then he let go of my collar, ready to tie the rope around me. This split second was my chance to get away.

As he stretched out the rope, ready to tie my hands, I sprang away from him and started to run. If I didn't make a dash through the trees I'd be finished. But the robber was faster than I thought. He caught hold of my arm, grasping it in his powerful hand and twisting it behind my back until I cried out. Then, pulling a stout stick from his pocket, he raised it up and brought it cracking down on my skull.

After that, everything went black.

When I woke from my dark dream, I found myself lying in the middle of the highway with needles of rain pricking at my face. My clothes were black with mud so I guessed that the stranger had dragged me out of the wood. He might have thought I was dead, or maybe not. I don't suppose he cared one way or the other.

My hands were bound with the rope and I was partly covered with the branch of a tree. Whoever came this way wouldn't see the rope and wouldn't realise it was a trick. I lay there thinking, *What to do? What to do?*

But as I twisted my hands, I found my wrists were not bound tightly at all. Could I slip my hands through the rope and get away? No, the man would be on me as soon as I stood up.

For some time I played dead; lying still but opening my eyes a little and peering through my eyelashes. I could see the stranger sitting at the foot of a beech tree a few paces off the road, leaning back against the trunk, waiting to hear the sound of a traveller approaching.

Instead, the noise that came was that of the horse, which was still tethered within the wood. He began to whinny, restless and wanting to be loose. He whinnied again louder now and I could hear him pawing at the ground.

'Useless creature, you are!' the man grumbled, getting to his feet. 'I'll be glad to be rid of you.' He walked in the direction of the horse, swishing his whip in his hand, and disappeared among the trees.

Now was the time to free myself. *Now!*

While he was away in the wood I twisted and turned, working my wrists, rubbing my skin raw in an effort to free myself. But I could not. Only when I felt a sharp stone on the ground, did I think I had a second chance. I began to rub the rope backwards and forward, over and over, until I felt it fray and finally break. Although one hand was free, the other was still fastened and the rope was tied round the beech tree.

Afraid that the villain would return at any second, I leaped up and ran to the edge of the wood letting the rope drape on the ground where it was almost invisible. I hid just in time before the man stomped back to the beech tree, glancing at the spot where he had left me. When he saw I was gone, his mouth fell open and he roared, 'Where are you, yer varmint?!' and ran towards the road.

He would have done well to look down at the ground for, as he ran, I pulled the rope tight and he tripped over it and fell spinning into a tree, cracking his head on the trunk so that he fell senseless to the ground.

With my free hand, I quickly untied the knot from my wrist and ran to where he lay. He was still breathing. How long would it be before he woke? I wondered. I wrapped the rope around him to secure it to the beech tree.

Before I could tie it his eyes shot open, fiery with rage, and he grabbed hold of my hand. I thought I was done for, but the fall had taken some of his strength. He couldn't hold me for long and I was able to twist out of his grip and wrench myself free. I ran off while he struggled to loosen the rope from his waist. I was away into the wood heading towards the horse.

I leaped onto his back and quickly untied him. Once he was free he needed no encouragement. He galloped away, with me knotting my fingers into his mane and hanging on for dear life. But the villain was already in our path, waving his arms and shouting, trying to stop us. But the horse did not stop. He rose up, soaring over his tormentor, his hooves knocking the man sideways as he flew through the air. And when he landed on the other side it was with such a crash that every bone in my body rattled.

But I held on. I was on the road to London.

Chapter 11
Rabbit Stew and No Shoes

The horse hurtled ahead through the driving rain. I clung on, grateful for the ride, knowing that my blistered feet wouldn't have got me very far.

All that day I rode, and the rain beat down relentlessly. After the long, hot summer, the world was turning to mud. The road was ankle deep in it and dotted with puddles. On and on we went until dusk by which time the horse was exhausted and had slowed to a plod. As for me, I was soaked and shivering. My clothes were clinging to me and water was running down my face and dripping off the end of my nose.

'I'm so hungry,' I said to the horse. 'We both need food and somewhere to rest for the night.'

I thought of Beth and the money hidden inside my doublet. 'Use it wisely – only when you need to,' she had said. Well, I needed to use it now. I was so ravenous that I could have eaten a rat.

We clomped along for another hour until we reached the outskirts of Uxbridge where I spotted a small inn set back from the road. A sign swung in the wind with the words BLACK BOAR painted on it. The inn was old, with rotting timbers and a thatched roof in need of repair. But smoke curled up from the chimneys and it looked warm and welcoming – I was desperate to go inside.

I slid off the horse and led him to the stables on the other side of a yard next to the inn. There were six stalls, empty except for two old nags.

'Penny for the night,' said a voice from the corner and I saw a scrawny boy, who I assumed must be the stable lad, crouching in the corner. 'Extra for the hay.'

I thought it was a lot to pay, but the horse was exhausted. He needed rest and food and so I took out the money and gave it to the stable lad.

I led the horse into a stall. 'Thank you, my friend,' I said, patting his mane and looking into his big brown eyes. 'You've looked after me well. You deserve a good supper and a rest before we leave tomorrow.' I went and fetched his hay and dropped it onto the floor of the stall. The horse lowered his head wearily and began to eat while I stroked his back for a time. Then, leaving him to have his fill, I walked across the yard to the Black Boar and pushed open the door.

I stepped into a smoke-filled room lit with tallow candles and warmed with a log fire that crackled in the hearth. The inn was crowded. People were laughing and shouting across the room. Some were drinking ale or shovelling food into their mouths. Most of them were soaked to the skin, like me, and the room was filled with the overwhelming stench of wet wool.

'Step inside, lad. There's a terrible draught,' someone called and I quickly shut the door behind me.

A serving wench threaded her way between the pine tables carrying two wooden trenchers of meat and bread, and the smell set my mouth watering and my stomach demanded to be filled. I pushed my way through the crowd and found the landlord leaning against the counter. He was a large man with a bulbous nose and a stomach bloated with too much food and drink.

'Could I have some supper, landlord?' I asked.

He fixed me with his rheumy eyes before belching loudly. 'Tuppence halfpenny,' he replied, his voice slurred with drink. 'No money, no food.' He held out his hand while I fetched more coins from my doublet and dropped them onto his palm.

I turned away, looking for somewhere to sit. 'Come and dry yourself by the fire,' beckoned an old man. 'There's a seat next to me.' And he moved along the bench to make room.

'Thank you, sir,' I said and flopped onto the bench and rested my head against its back.

The old man nodded and smiled while I toasted in the heat of the burning logs. It wasn't long before my fingers and toes began to tingle and my cheeks flushed pink. It was a good feeling and I soon felt drowsy and my eyelids closed. I fell to dreaming of soft mattresses and woollen blankets.

It was the old man who woke me with a sharp dig to my ribs. 'See to, lad,' he said. 'The wench has fetched your trencher. And a lovely looking wench she is, for sure.' He nudged me again, and I rubbed my eyes.

When I looked up I saw a girl not much older than me standing by the table. She had a mass of long red hair, blue eyes, and cheeks painted red. She was holding a tankard of ale in one hand and a plate of stew in the other.

I sat up straight as she put them in front of me. 'Thank you,' I said and she bobbed a curtsey.

The old man was staring at her and he leaned forward as she walked past and slapped her buttocks, making her squeal.

'Bonny lass, eh?' he chuckled, nudging me again.

The maid dodged away but four rowdy farmers at the next table had their eyes on her too. They shouted coarse comments and one of them grabbed hold of her.

'How now, pretty wench,' he cried, squeezing her tight. 'Come, give this farmer a kiss with those fine rosy lips of yours.'

He pulled her towards him and she said, 'How now, sir?' as primly as you like but somehow managed to knock his tankard so that ale spilled over his lap, soaking his breeches. Then, still smiling, she raised her foot and stamped hard on his toes, leaving him howling in pain while his farmer friends laughed and slapped him on the back as she walked away.

I settled down to eat the rabbit stew which was the most delicious I had ever tasted and I mopped up every last drop of gravy with my bread. For the first time in days my stomach was full and I was satisfied.

Now I was ready for sleep.

The red-faced landlord came staggering over to the fire with an armful of logs.

'Excuse me, sir,' I called to him. 'I should like to stay the night.'

He bent forward and tossed the logs one by one onto the fire before turning to look at me.

'The feather bed is taken,' he sniffed as he wiped his hands on his apron. 'There is a straw mattress for tuppence or you can sleep on the floor for a penny, if you will.'

I had already spent most of Beth's money and thought it best to save where I could. I would need the rest to see me through the first few days in London.

'Thank you, landlord. The floor will be good enough. I should like to sleep now, if I may.' I stood up and stepped towards him.

He grunted. 'And there'll be a halfpenny for a candle.' He held out his great hand while I felt inside my doublet and produced two coins.

The landlord walked uncertainly across the room, bumping into his customers as he went. When he reached the counter, he passed me a candle stick. 'Up there,' he said, nodding towards the stairs.

I climbed wearily up to the bedchamber and held the candle high above my head and looked around the room. It was square with a low-beamed ceiling and stank of sweat and dirty bedding. In the far corner there was a bed and next to it was a piss pot in need of emptying. By the wall, arranged in a row, there were four mattresses. The one by the window was already occupied by a man with a rough black beard who was lying on his back, his mouth open, snoring like a pig in a sty. The only free space I could lie in was by the door where an old woollen blanket had been left in a heap.

I put my candle on the floor and sat down. I did not like to take off my clothes – even though they were still damp – for fear they might be stolen. But my shoes were a different matter. I had to remove them for the blisters on my heels were very painful. Slowly, I eased them off my feet and then I lay down, holding them tight to my chest in case of thieves. I pulled the blanket over me, glad of its warmth even though it was flea-ridden and drove me mad with itching.

It wasn't long before I fell asleep but I was woken soon after when the door of the bedchamber swung open. *Crash!* It hammered against my back and I opened my eyes to see a tall bruiser of a man stagger into the room. Unsteady after too much ale, he tripped over me and fell to the floor, cursing.

'What heap is this?' he roared as he scrambled to his feet. 'Get out of my way!' And he kicked me hard on my legs with his great boot. He struck me several more times for good measure before stumbling across the room and collapsing onto the bed, too drunk to cover himself.

Not long afterwards, a coarse pair of ruffians burst in, filling the room with the stink of their breath. They spent an hour or more repeating crude jokes and laughing so loudly that, tired as I was, I couldn't sleep. Only when they finally went silent and shut their eyes, did I close mine and I didn't open them until the light of dawn.

When I woke, the room was empty. All four men must have left early, I thought. I stood up and stretched the stiffness out of my bones before moving to put on my shoes. But I couldn't find them. I looked under the blanket. I looked all around the room but they were nowhere to be seen. My shoes, which I remembered clutching to my chest, were gone.

In a panic, I suddenly remembered my money. I felt inside my doublet, first one side and then the other. There was nothing. Not a penny. Not a farthing. While I was sleeping everything had been stolen.

Chapter 12
No Job for a Girl

I raced downstairs looking for help and saw the landlord rolling a barrel of ale through the door of the inn. 'Landlord!' I shouted. 'Someone has stolen my money and my shoes.'

He settled the barrel upright as I ran over to him and looked at me, scowling. 'What can I do about it?' His breath stank of ale. 'You must have left them somewhere foolish.'

'No, sir. I had my shoes close to my chest and the money was inside my doublet.'

He poured himself a tankard of beer and downed it in one. 'Inside your doublet?' he scoffed as he wiped froth from his lips. 'Well, well. If that is so, boy, it was a clever thief who took 'em.'

As far as he was concerned, my problem had nothing to do with him. He filled his tankard again and took it with him as he walked unsteadily through the door. That left me alone except for the serving wench scrubbing the tables.

Not knowing what to do, I slumped in a chair pressing my hand on my forehead.

'You in trouble?' asked the girl. 'I heard what you said just then.'

I nodded and glanced up at her. She had stopped her work and was leaning on the table, her hand on the scrubbing brush and her flame-coloured hair hanging over her face which was now washed clear of the red paint.

'I'm in real trouble,' I replied.

Then she stood up, tossing back her hair and I saw that her eyes were swollen from crying and her cheek was badly bruised.

'I ain't surprised,' she said. 'This place is full of thieves and vagabonds. I'd go back home tomorrow, if I could.'

'Where's your home?'

'London. Ma sent me here to earn a living and to keep away from the plague.'

'Don't you like your work?'

Her blue eyes flashed and her cheeks flushed pink. '*Like it?* What do you think?' She began scrubbing angrily in frantic circles, gritting her teeth. 'I don't like it one little bit.'

'Why?'

'Cos the landlord tells me I have a sharp tongue and I offend his customers. So he beats me.'

I shrugged my shoulders. 'I get beaten at school but I've got used to it.'

She stopped the scrubbing and frowned. 'I ain't a donkey, am I?' she snapped, waving the scrubbing brush at me. 'Must I be tormented by them ruffians? Must I be made to paint my face like a doll to please, 'em? I'm too ashamed to tell you how they treats a girl. The landlord says I must put up with it. But I'd rather risk the plague – that's the honest truth!'

She told me her name was Alice and that her family lived by Cripplegate. I told her of my plan to seek my fortune.

'Master Kemp has asked me to visit him at the Curtain and then I shall join William Shakespeare's troupe and become an actor.' This was not strictly speaking the truth. But as I was talking to a complete stranger, what did it matter?

'William Shakespeare?' she said, suddenly brightening and grinning at me. 'I have seen him at the Curtain. Ma and me went there. Oh, I remember... It was wonderful.'

'So you've seen some plays?'

'Lots. Do you know my favourite?'

'What is it?'

'*Romeo and Juliet.*'

'Never heard of it.'

'It's really exciting,' she said, settling on the edge of a table. 'Juliet wants to marry Romeo, see, but her father won't let her.'

Another play about love. I wasn't interested. But there was no stopping Alice.

'Well then she goes and takes a sleeping potion. Oh, it's terrible! Her parents think she's dead, they do.'

Alice slipped off the table. 'Listen to this, Thomas. You'll like it.' And she stepped into the middle of the room, placing her hands dramatically across her chest before speaking the lines.

'*How if, when I am laid into the tomb,*
I wake before the time that Romeo
Come to redeem me?'

'Is that Juliet?' I asked and she nodded. 'You're very good, Alice!'

70

'I can't read nor nothink, but I remember words. Ma says my memory is a wonder!' She skipped back to the table. 'One day I should like to play Juliet on the stage and wear a fine gown with the audience clapping an' all.' Then she suddenly looked miserable. 'Instead, I scrub tables and serve drunken louts.'

I shook my head. 'Acting is no life for girls, Alice. They are not allowed on the stage.'

She stood up straight with her hands on her hips. 'I know it ain't allowed! But why ain't it? Why can't a girl play a girl's part?'

'Because it would be shameful.'

'Oh!' she screeched, 'And is it not shameful for a girl of fourteen to be poked at and have her bottom pinched by men who should know better?'

Not knowing how to reply, I said, 'I have to go,' and limped towards the door, conscious of my bare feet.

'Can I come with you?' Alice called after me. 'If I find you a pair of boots, will you let me come?'

At the word 'boots' I stopped and turned round.

She grinned at me. 'A girl ain't safe travelling on her own, see. But I'd be safe with you, Thomas. I'll bring some food, if you like.'

She seemed a good sort and it wasn't such a bad idea to have company on the road to London. So I agreed that we would travel together.

'My horse can take the two of us on his back.'

'You got a horse?' she asked, her eyes widening in surprise.

And when I said that I had, she told me to go to the stables and wait there for her.

'I'll come as soon as I can get away without nobody seeing,' she said and shooed me outside.

Chapter 13
London Wall

As I walked out of the inn I was glad to see that the rain had stopped. I crossed the yard to the stables, looking forward to seeing the black horse now he was well rested and fed. He had been a good friend to me. Yesterday he had saved my life and now he would take Alice and me to London.

I opened the stable door but, as I stepped inside, my blood ran cold. The stable boy – if that what was he was – was nowhere to be seen. The stables were empty. The old nags had gone and so had the black horse. The fine animal that had brought me this far had been stolen. I sank to the floor with my head in my hands. I should have expected it. My shoes and money had been stolen – why not the horse?

Feeling wretched, I waited for Alice. I crouched in the first stall, watching through a crack in the wall. It was some time before I saw her running across the yard, holding her skirt off the ground, her red hair flying behind her. She was carrying a wicker basket and I hoped it was filled with food for the journey.

She burst through the door. 'We'd best go before the landlord sees what I've done,' she said, grinning with excitement until she saw my miserable face. 'What's up?' she asked.

I pointed at the empty stall. 'They've taken the horse too.'

'The rogues!' Alice replied. 'But I wouldn't put nothink past 'em!'

'We'll have to walk,' I said.

'No. We'll have to run! When the old toad sees I've got his best boots he'll go ravin' mad. And when he finds I've run off with his cheese and pies...oh heavens above.' She threw her head back and laughed. 'Anyway, I'm not such a thief. He ain't paid me no wages.' She tugged at my sleeve. 'Shame about the horse, Thomas, but don't hang about. That landlord's got a terrible temper.'

Once we were well away from the inn, we slowed our pace. The day was dull and the road muddy from yesterday's rain but Alice strode out, excited to be heading home. Even when her skirts grew sodden and blackened round the hem she never complained.

'I'll be glad to see Ma and my brothers,' she told me. 'I had six brothers, I did. But two of 'em died of the smallpox. Pa died too. We was lucky that we didn't catch it, Ma said. The queen herself nearly died of it.'

I was wearing the landlord's boots. Better than bare feet, you might think. But the landlord was a giant of a man and his boots were enormous so that my poor blistered feet slithered around inside. By midday my skin was rubbed raw and I could only limp along.

'Pity your feet ain't as big as his,' Alice laughed as I sat on the side of the road wiping the blood off my toes with my shirt.

'What you need is some padding,' she suggested. Then she lifted her skirt and tore strips off her petticoat. 'Wrap 'em round yer toes, Thomas. That'll pack out the boots, see.'

Bandaged, my feet felt much more comfortable and, before we set off again, we rested for a while and ate one of the pies Alice had stolen from the Black Boar.

'Delicious!' I said, sinking my teeth into the pastry.

'Not so good as you'll find in London,' Alice boasted, and she leaned forward, peering down the road as if she could already see the city.

'The mile stone back there said ten miles to London,' I told her when I'd finished the pie. 'We should get there before dark.'

Alice stood up and brushed the crumbs off her skirt. 'We'll have to hurry, Thomas. The gates will be shut and locked at dusk.'

'Shut?'

'Aye. We won't be allowed through until the morning. Come on.'

I wiped my mouth and clambered to my feet, setting off after her as fast as I could.

The nearer we got to London, the busier the road became. It grew so crowded that we were crushed among men on horseback with panniers full of apples and pears, and farmers driving flocks of geese and sheep. Stratford was never like this.

We had gone a good distance but Alice kept looking up at the darkening sky, afraid that the light was fading fast.

'Can't you walk no quicker, Thomas?' she said. 'The gates will be locked before long.' She glanced over her shoulder and when she saw a cart heading our way she held up her hand to the driver.

'Good day, kind sir!' she called as he came close. 'Can we beg a ride? My friend has injured his feet.'

'Full load,' the driver shouted and passed straight on without even a sideways glance.

Alice stamped her foot and shook her fist. 'May your wheels drop off!' she yelled as the cart disappeared into the distance.

But our luck changed when another came along. It was pulled by an old grey mare and driven by a man in a white smock who sat with his head lolling on his chest as if he were asleep. His wife – a large lady of at least forty – was at his side talking incessantly and munching on an apple.

Alice nudged me. 'See that!' she said nodding at the cart. 'Just watch and catch up.'

As the cart passed us by Alice ran after it, grasping hold of the side before jumping onto the back and beckoning me to follow. Luckily the horse moved at a slow pace on account of her age so I was able catch up in spite of my sore feet. We had plenty of room to sit side by side as the cart was only half full with sacks of apples and pears. We dangled our feet over the back watching the world go by and munching on the fruit. Without doubt, this was the way to travel.

We had gone a mile or more when the driver's wife happened to turn round to reach for a pear. Of course she spotted us.

'Oi!' she yelled. 'What you doin'? Pinching our goods! Get off my cart, you filthy young vagabonds.' She poked her husband with her elbow. 'Joshua! Wake up! We've got company.'

The cart came to a sudden halt and the wife leaped off, wielding a horse whip. 'I'll have you!' she shouted, but, before she could reach us, we had jumped down and set off running.

'Over there!' I yelled to Alice, pointing at a farmer driving a herd of cows to market.

We ran towards the cattle and hid amongst them so we couldn't be seen. The woman with the whip looked about her, but when she failed to spot us she lost interest and climbed back onto the cart, muttering to her husband as they started off again.

Others passed us. More than I could count.

'Everyone's going to London,' said Alice. ''Tis the busiest place in the world.' And not long after, she suddenly squealed, 'Look, Thomas! Look!' and bounced up and down pointing ahead. 'There it is. That's London.'

I followed the direction of her finger expecting to see a town like Stratford, but bigger. What I saw was an ancient wall with a vast encampment of hovels and workshops and rough buildings propped up against it.

'That's London?'

'No,' she said, punching my arm. 'That's London Wall. There's a wall right around the City, see.'

'A wall? Then how do we get in?'

'Through Newgate. Come quick, Thomas, for it will be closed soon.'

The road took us over a stinking river but once we'd passed it, Newgate itself came into view. I stopped and stood gaping, for it was not a gate as I knew a gate to be. It was not a wooden thing in a field that swung on hinges. No. It was a building that looked like a castle – or what I thought a castle should look like. It was built of stone, with a tower on either side of a large gateway that led into the city. There was a stream of people hurrying out of London, and a queue of people trying to get in. They were carrying sacks, driving carts and riding horses. The people going in jostled with the people coming out, making the most terrible crush I had ever seen.

'Don't stand there staring, Thomas,' Alice called over her shoulder. 'Hurry or we shall never get through in time.'

I limped after her pushing through the crowd as best I could, and we were almost at the gate when church bells began to ring all over the city, filling the skies with a heavenly noise.

'Amazing!' I said and stood still listening. 'I wish Beth could hear this.'

But Alice glowered at me. 'Hens' teeth, Thomas! It's not amazing – it's the curfew!'

She grabbed my arm, desperate to get into the city, but, as the bells faded, we saw the huge gates swing closed.

'No!' she yelled and stamped her foot, furious to have missed the gate by a whisker.

'That's bad luck,' I said.

Alice looked as if she could kill me. 'Bad luck? Bad luck?' she yelled. 'We could be murdered in our sleep while we squat among the ruffians by the wall. Very bad luck indeed, I'd say.'

I tried to calm her temper. 'We passed over a river back there,' I said, pointing the way we had come. 'We could sit on the bank and soak our feet.'

Alice raised her eyebrows. 'Don't you know nothink?' she snapped, her blue eyes flashing. 'All the butchers and slaughtermen dump cows' heads and rotting carcasses there. That is the Fleet River, if you didn't know it. If you gets near, your nose will drop off with the stink.' She turned her back on me and folded her arms. 'So I won't be putting my feet in it, thank you very much!'

As the day darkened, the wall of London city glowed with small fires lit by travellers to keep themselves warm through the night. We threaded our way past groups of them as we looked for a space big enough to sit and rest till morning. Some folks were making merry with jugs of ale. Some called out to us, yelling and laughing and using lewd language as we passed.

'Hey, lassie,' shouted one of a group of men sitting around a fire. 'Come and drink with us, eh? You'll not regret it, pretty maid.'

He stood up and staggered towards Alice, snatching hold of her arm.

'Leave me be!' she shouted and struggled to get away but, as she did, her feet slipped on the muddy ground and she fell. 'I'd rather drink with the devil!' she screamed and kicked out at his legs and spat at him. He leaned over her, laughing, but she reached up, scratching at his face with her fingernails.

I frantically searched around for something to strike him with and found a piece of timber. While Alice tried to fight off the rogue, I stepped up behind him, lifted the wood high and swung it at his head. *Bang!* He was knocked off balance and went sprawling into the mud. His companions roared with laughter at his downfall but left him to lie where he fell.

I helped Alice to her feet and, as we ran away, someone shouted, 'Well done, boy!'

When I looked to my right, I saw a man, tall as a mountain, with dark skin and black curly hair, leaning against the wall. He was wearing a leather apron and had muscles like turnips.

'You and your sister come by me,' he called, gesturing to us. 'You stay here.'

The man told us he was a blacksmith. He must have worked hard for he shoed horses, mended pans and made knives. His was a thriving business not far from the gate.

'You stay by my forge,' he insisted. 'Nobody will dare to bother you while I'm around.' Then he looked over to the group of troublesome men and raised a clenched fist, sending a message that they all understood.

We were grateful for the kindness of the blacksmith for he showed us a good space between the wall and the forge where we settled down feeling warm and safe – until Alice suddenly sat bolt upright.

'Oh great heaven, Thomas!' she cried. 'I've lost my basket and it's got the cheese in it! I must have gone and dropped it by them men. I'll have to get it back.'

'No. Leave it, Alice,' I replied, tugging at her arm. 'What matters a cheese? Tomorrow we shall be in London.' Too tired to argue, she flopped down again, and fell fast asleep.

It was not long before the people camping by the wall let

their fires die out, ceased their chatter and lay down. But I tossed and turned for an hour or more, unable to sleep for the terrible noises coming from Newgate. Screaming and yelling and moaning. Noises like I had never heard.

I nudged Alice.

'What's all that din?' I asked.

She half opened her eyes. 'Just ignore 'em, Thomas. It's only the prisoners in Newgate. Noisy lot.'

'What do you mean "prisoners"?' I said, but I didn't get an answer. So I lay on my back gazing at the stars and waiting for the dawn when I would walk into the great city of London to find fame, fortune and Master Shakespeare.

London

Chapter 14
The Trowte House

The next morning, before the sun broke through, the black-smith shouted to us to wake up. The forge was glowing in readiness for the day's work and he was standing by his anvil, a hammer in his hand.

'The gate will be open soon, young-'uns,' he called cheer-fully. 'The queue is already forming. Best be on your way.'

We got to our feet, rubbing the sleep from our eyes, and thanked the blacksmith for his kindness.

'May good fortune follow you,' he said, smiling his wide, white smile and waving farewell as we set off towards Newgate.

Once we had joined the queue to the enter the city, Alice said, 'We'll go to my house first, Thomas. I can't wait to see Ma.'

For a second I thought of my own family and wished that I could see them. But when Alice said, 'Then I'll take you to the Curtain,' the homesickness quickly disappeared.

There must have been a hundred people or more wanting to pass through Newgate. And when it swung open there was a good deal of pushing and shoving but eventually we walked through.

London! Here I was at last.

The first thing I noticed was the noise. Street traders were shouting their wares. 'Apples. Ripe apples.' 'Come sharpen your knives.' 'Milko! Milko!' 'Sweep! Chimney sweep!' People were jostling along the street while carts rumbled over the cobbles, their wheels creaking and grinding. Skinny dogs barked and sheep bleated as they were driven to market. Carpenters in their leather aprons carried timber over their shoulders and called, 'Make way! Make way!' as they tried to pass. I never thought so many people could be crammed into one place.

And the houses! They were packed tight together along narrow streets with their upper floors projecting so far that someone in a bedchamber could reach out of the window and shake hands with his neighbour in the house opposite.

Alice slapped me on the back. 'Ain't it a fine place, Thomas? Ain't it a deal better than the country, eh?'

Was London better? I couldn't be sure, for it was not only crowded and noisy, it was also dirty and extremely smelly. Black smoke billowed from the metalworking shops and belched out of the chimneys of the houses. There was a terrible stink from the sewer channel that ran down the middle of the road – much worse than anything we had in Stratford. Even the cobbles were slippery with human waste and rotting rubbish that had been slung into the street.

I pinched my nose and turned to Alice. 'Does nobody clear up the mess?' I asked.

She laughed. 'No! Why would we be doing that? We got dogs and pigs and kites, ain't we? They'll take it all in good time.'

Then she suddenly grabbed my arm and pulled me aside as a rooting pig, its snout covered in slime, knocked against me on its way to feed off the rubbish. 'See!' she said. 'He'll have a fine meal of what's lying around.'

We left the pig to its dinner and turned off the main street into a warren of alleyways, mud instead of cobbles underfoot now. Each one of them was narrower than the last, with little room for daylight to squeeze in. Alice led the way, and turned at the corner where a wooden sign in the shape of a boot swung overhead. It reminded me of Father and set me wondering if he was thinking about me.

'This way!' shouted Alice. 'Catch up, Thomas.' We were in the narrowest and darkest alley of all, and when she reached the top she stopped in front of a rotting door and beckoned me to come.

'This is it,' she called, grinning with excitement.

She pushed open the door and I followed her into a small, dark room which was lit by the stub of a tallow candle on a table. Alice's mother, who looked much older than I expected, was sitting by an empty grate holding a tankard of ale. She was dressed in what I guessed were her dead husband's shirt and jerkin – torn and grubby like her skirt. On her feet she wore a pair of ancient boots tied with string with holes cut out to ease her bunions.

'Ma! It's me,' Alice called as she stepped nearer. 'I'm back.'

Mother Trowte looked up and stared at us. 'Is that you, girl?' she said, squeezing her eyes to see us better. 'Thought you was working in the country? Come and give your mother a kiss.' Alice flung her arms around her ma's shoulders and planted a kiss on her wrinkled cheek. 'I've brought a visitor.'

Her mother turned and stared at me. 'And who's he?' she said as if I had crawled out of a hole in the ground. 'You ain't in no trouble, is you, girl?'

'No, Ma. This is Thomas. He wants to be famous. He's come to find Will Kemp, the actor.'

'And William Shakespeare,' I added.

Her mother looked puzzled, shaking her head as if she didn't understand. Alice leaned forward and put her hand on her arm. 'You remember, Ma. At the Curtain in Shoreditch. That play we saw.'

Suddenly the old woman slapped her knee and threw her head back laughing, revealing gums with just one crooked tooth hanging precariously in the middle. 'Ah! I remember,' she chuckled. 'We had a good time, eh, Alice?' Then she looked across at me sharply. 'But what you doin' looking for Will Kemp, boy? That won't do you no good.'

'I want to be an actor, mistress, and maybe write plays one day.'

Mother Trowte pressed her gums together and wagged her finger at me. 'You don't want to go mixing with them types,' she said. 'Villains! That's what they are. Villains!' She leaned forward confidentially. 'You heard about Ben Johnson?'

'Is he an actor?'

'He's a writer, so they say. He mixes with the likes of Will Shakespeare. They're all as bad as each other,' she said, taking a swig of ale and wiping her mouth on her sleeve. 'That Ben Johnson's got a wicked temper, I hear. Last week he was in a fight with one of them actors over by Hoxton Fields. Stabbed him, he did.'

'No!' Alice gasped.

'Oh, ah. Killed him dead as mutton. Now Ben Johnson's in Newgate – where he should be, if you ask me. I expect he'll hang.' She pointed a bony finger at me. 'I'm telling you, my lad. You stay away from them writers and actors. Find yourself proper work.'

'Well, that's a fine welcome an' no mistake, Ma. Won't you offer us a bite to eat?'

'We've got some of yesterday's bread,' she replied, nodding towards a loaf on the table. 'You can have that.'

Alice tore off a piece and handed it to me.

'I'm glad you're home, girl,' said Mother Trowte as she settled back in her chair and took a mouthful of ale. 'Things is hard. I can't work no more and our Nathanial and Nicholas have left home.'

'Why did they do that?'

'Joined Her Majesty's navy. Off to the Spanish Main to seek their fortune, they said. I expect they was thinking of Spanish treasure – but if you asks me, they won't find any. Things ain't what they used to be.' She shook her head and chewed on her bottom lip. 'It was different when Sir Francis Drake was in charge. He could show them foreigners a thing or two.'

'He's dead now, Ma.'

'More's the pity,' the old lady snapped. 'Them Spaniards are still making mischief, and it is said there are plots to kill the queen. Can you believe it?'

Alice tried to change the subject. 'What about Jack and Willum? Have they been looking after you, Ma?'

'Not so well, girl. They was earning good money from them leather tanners, collecting dog dung from the streets here about. Two buckets a day they got.' She paused, lifted her skirt and gave her legs a good scratching to ease her flea bites. 'They was doin' all right until old Percy Pimble come round. He starts shouting and blathering that they was on his pitch and he told 'em to clear off, or else. So that was the end of that.'

'Where are they now?' asked Alice, looking around.

'Out thieving at the market,' Ma Trowte replied. 'But they're not much good at it. Yesterday they only come home with a couple of pears.'

We stayed for a while, Alice chatting excitedly with her mother, telling her how glad she was to be back in London. But when I felt fleas leaping off Mother Trowte and attacking my neck, hopping south beneath my shirt, I thought it was time to go. I gave Alice a knowing look and I was relieved when she said, 'I'll take Thomas over to Shoreditch, Ma, and I'll come back with something to eat.' Then she gave her mother a big hug and we turned to leave.

I was one step nearer to my new life.

Chapter 15

Turnips on Spikes

'I'll show you the way across the city,' said Alice, shutting the door behind us. 'We'll go out through Bishopsgate.'

I grabbed hold of her arm. 'What do you mean – go out of London? Master Kemp said I should meet him *in* London because Master Shakespeare lives *in* London and the Chamberlain's Men are *in* London. What are you talking about, Alice?'

Alice tossed her head. 'You don't know nothin', do you, Thomas Munmore?' she said, pushing my hand away. 'Acting ain't allowed inside the city walls and the Curtain's in Shoreditch which is just outside, if you must know. So don't blow yourself into a fit.'

Then she spun round and skipped ahead while I limped behind her. She was as chirpy as a sparrow, holding her skirt off the ground and singing at the top of her voice.

'Now is the month of Maying,
When merry lambs are playing.
Fa la lalalalalala,
Fa la lalalala.'

It was stupid singing a song like that. It wasn't May. It was September, and what lamb would play in the dismal, dark alleyways of London? Only when we turned into Cheapside was the road wide enough to let the sun shine through.

I was surprised to see fine houses – on that road – some five-storeys high – and shops on either side, each one with a colourful sign creaking and swinging over it. The Black Bear. The Leg. The Red Cross. Further along there were rows of apothecaries' shops where potions and remedies were mixed, and then there were grocers selling spices and herbs, filling the air with sweet smells, which was a welcome change from the London stink.

Suddenly Alice stopped. 'See over there?' she said, looking towards a large stone building some way ahead. 'That's Bishopsgate. You go through there and you'll soon be at Shoreditch. Come on. I'll go with you to the gate and then I'll go home. I want to pick up a rabbit at the market. The little-'uns will like that.'

'But you've no money, Alice.'

'I know,' she laughed, nudging me with her elbow. 'Till I gets work, I'll have to do a bit o' thieving, won't I? Needs must, as Ma would say.'

Alice was so happy to be back in London that she pranced and sang all the way down the road, waving her arms in the air like branches in a breeze. We soon reached Bishopsgate, which was a fine old building similar to Newgate but not so grand. It was made of stone with a large gate in the middle. Above it I noticed two huge turnips stuck on spikes.

'There's a funny thing,' I said, pointing upwards. 'Why would anyone put turnips up there?'

'Turnips?' asked Alice following my gaze. Then she burst out laughing as if I had said something very funny. 'Them ain't turnips. Ain't you never seen villains' heads, Thomas? We sees 'em regular in London.'

I gawked at what I'd thought were vegetables and realised that they were two gruesome heads with tongues lolling from their gaping mouths and blood dripping from their severed necks. I grimaced and looked away.

Alice looked up at them, her head cocked to one side and her hands on her hips. 'Those heads are fresh, by the looks of 'em,' she said, telling me what I didn't want to know. 'If they'd been there for a day or two the crows would have picked their eyes out.'

Feeling queasy I trailed after her through the gate until she stopped. 'The Curtain's that way,' she stabbed the air with her finger. 'Follow your nose for half a mile, past the old monastery gardens, and you'll find it.'

'Thank you, Alice. You've been a great help,' I said. 'Shall we meet again?'

Alice grinned. 'We may, one day. You never know,' she said and started walking backwards, calling, 'Goodbye, Thomas. Goodbye. You'll be famous in no time. Mark my words.'

Then she spun round and ran back through Bishopsgate, her hair tossing in the wind.

Chapter 16
The White Hart

On the other side of Bishopsgate I saw the poorest hovels set against the London Wall, and further on, tumbledown cottages spreading through fields and marches. As I walked away from the city, many travellers were heading towards it. Some were on foot, some on horseback, some with carts packed full of fruit for market. It was a busy road. But, just as Alice had said, once I had passed the ruins of the old monastery, it wasn't long before I reached the Curtain.

Now I was so near I was all of a tremble and stood at the side of the road staring at the playhouse, worrying what Master Kemp would say when he saw me again. Would he be pleased? Would he be angry? And most of all I wondered, would Master Shakespeare himself be there?

By then, my knees were knocking and refused to stop. But there was no point in standing there. With my heart pounding against my ribs, I walked unsteadily towards the door of the Curtain and entered.

The playhouse was empty apart from five young apprentices who were kicking a pig's bladder, blown up fit to burst, round the floor. As I entered, they stopped and stared at me.

'Who are you?' one shouted. 'What you doing in here?'

I recognised them from the play in Stratford. They had been the fairies and one had been a love-sick girl.

I pulled myself up to my full height and said, 'I'm Thomas Munmore and I've come to speak to Master Kemp.'

'Have yer?' said a round-faced boy with curly hair. 'Well, he ain't here, so get back to where you belong.'

The five of them walked towards me in a threatening manner and I was about to run when I heard the door open and someone walk in. It was the same spotty, dark-haired boy I had seen at Stratford collecting money for the play.

'Who are you?' he asked.

'He's nobody,' yelled one of the other boys.

'Come to see Master Kemp, so he said.'

The spotty boy stared at me. 'I know you, don't I? Stratford, weren't it? You was talking to Master Kemp about that ass's head. I remember.'

I grinned and felt a sense of relief flood over me. The mood in the room had suddenly changed. 'He asked me to come to London and join the Chamberlain's Men,' I said, stretching the truth. But what did it matter?

On hearing this, the apprentices burst out laughing and jeering until the older boy spun round and shut them up with a stern look.

'He asked you to come, did he?'

'Yes. My name is Thomas Munmore.'

'Well, Thomas Munmore, Master Kemp's always inviting people, see. Everywhere we goes, he invites 'em. That's actors for yer. He don't mean nothink by it. Don't mean a thing. He's most likely forgotten.'

My shoulders drooped and I felt sick to the stomach.

'I'd go back home if I was you. We've got plenty of apprentice actors. Don't need no more.'

If he had slapped me in the face I couldn't have been more shocked. Had I come all this way for nothing? If I went home, I'd be clapped in gaol before you could say Stratford-upon-Avon.

The boy walked with me to the door and stepped outside. My face must have said it all.

'Run away from home, have yer?'

I didn't have the strength to lie. I just nodded.

'Father beat you, did he?'

'No!' I protested. Then I confessed, 'I was seen poaching.'

'Ah! So you're in trouble with the law, eh?'

I nodded again.

'No going back then? No money?'

I shook my head.

'Well, Thomas, I've been in the same situation myself, see. So I'll give you a tip.' He looked at me and winked. 'In a couple of hours you come back and stand outside the Curtain.'

'How will that help?'

He grinned. 'All them rich folk with horses need somebody to hold 'em, see. You'll get paid for it – not much but it'll pay for a meal and a bed in the stables at the White Hart.' He nudged me. 'Don't want to go hungry, do yer? Don't want to sleep in a ditch?'

'No, I don't,' I said and thanked him for his advice.

'My name's Roger. Dare say I'll see you around the place.' He walked back into the playhouse.

So, that first day in London, I earned a few farthings by standing outside the Curtain taking care of two bay mares until the play was finished and the owners returned.

Roger was a good sort. When he'd swept up after the afternoon's performance he took me down to the White Hart where he was going to eat his dinner. The inn was not far away, set back from the road and built of timber and thatch. There was just one square room, already crowded with travellers, the air thick with wood smoke.

Roger elbowed his way across to a large table, where a group of men were deep in conversation.

'Master Kemp,' Roger called above the hubbub of the tavern. 'That boy from Stratford-upon-Avon has come to see you. He's here, sir.'

The conversation stopped and eight pairs of eyes turned to look at me.

'This is Thomas Munmore. He's the lad who told you how to make a better ass's head for yourself.' And Roger grinned and bowed low in a mocking fashion.

Will Kemp, sitting at the far end, stood up and flung his arms wide. 'Well, well, well, Thomas Munmore, I do not remember your face but you are welcome to eat with us. Come! Join us!'

Could it be that he had forgotten me already? I felt foolish as I sat down at the table.

Roger leaned towards Will Kemp. 'He says you invited him to join our company.' And I saw him wink and some of the others tittered.

Master Kemp stared at me and squeezed his eyes to get a

better look. I blushed with embarrassment. My lie had been found out.

But before I could say a word a man at the other end of the table spoke, his voice deep and filled with sadness. 'You say you have forgotten this boy's face, Will, but I have not.'

Everyone turned to look at him.

'I know this boy,' he continued. 'I met him in my garden at New Place. He is the very image of my son, Hamnet. How could I forget? A fine boy. A fine boy.'

William Shakespeare himself was not an arm's length away. Seeing him again like this, I could hardly breathe. He looked just as grand with his clipped beard and his gold earring. To me, even his hands were perfect, stained as they were with black ink. I couldn't take my eyes off him.

'I am pleased to see you again, Thomas. But how did you get here?' he asked. 'It is a long way from Stratford.'

I told him how I had to flee from Clopton's men and how I walked some of the way and rode some of the way on a stolen horse. And how I had spent the past few hours holding mares outside the theatre.

Master Shakespeare stood up, clapping his hands. ''Tis well done, Thomas. Well done, for that is the story of my youth. I went poaching when I was a lad and had to run for my life or face the hangman.' Then he turned to speak to the others around the table. 'This boy has a good deal of courage. I wish that my own son had the chance to grow such pluck.' Everyone was silent. 'You have a dream to become an actor? Is that right, Thomas?'

'It is, sir.'

He looked at the others around the table. 'I should like us to take this fine boy into our troupe. Are you gentlemen in agreement?' I held my breath while the group muttered their approval and nodded their heads. Then Master Shakespeare turned to me with his heavy, sad eyes. 'I regret that we have no need of actors, Thomas, but until we do, you may help in other ways and earn your keep.'

'Thank you, sir. I will work hard.'

'Make me proud, Thomas,' he said, resting his hand on my shoulder as a father might do to his son. 'I know you won't let me down.' Then he spoke to the others. 'Gentleman, I must leave you.' He took a last mouthful of ale. 'I have business to attend to.' And with that, he strode towards the door and left the inn.

I could hardly speak for the excitement of knowing I was to be a part of the Chamberlain's Men, and when Master Kemp ordered me a plate of mutton I gobbled it down for my stomach had seen no food since the piece of bread at Ma Trowte's house.

When I had done he leaned towards me and said, 'You were lucky to find the Chamberlain's Men at the Curtain, Thomas. We returned only two days ago and this was our first performance after a summer travelling the countryside. I am glad to be back in London. There is no place like it.'

I nodded. 'Indeed, sir,' I said, wiping my mouth on the back of my hand. 'London is a fine city.'

'And what of your family?' he asked. 'Do they know you have come to join us?'

I hesitated, not knowing whether to tell him the truth. 'My family is in Stratford, sir. My sister knows I wish to act more than anything,' I replied (which was not a lie). 'I've dreamed about it for a long time.'

'Perhaps one day you will. First, you must write to your family to tell them you are safe. Your letters will go with Master Shakespeare's when he writes to his wife. You know already that she lives in Stratford-upon-Avon.'

'I do, sir,' I said, and was relieved that he did not ask more questions which might be difficult to answer.

'You will do very well, I'm sure, Thomas. Let us shake on it.' Master Kemp gripped my hand so enthusiastically that I thought my fingers would break. But in spite of the pain I was bursting with happiness.

'Where shall I sleep, sir?' I asked.

He smiled and pointed to a dapper man with clipped hair sitting further down the table. 'Mr Heminge is our manager,' he explained. 'He will see to lodgings. You'll be well looked after.'

And so I began my life with the Chamberlain's Men – though I had no idea then of the danger it would lead me into.

Chapter 17

The Start of a Dream

Life with the Chamberlain's Men began smoothly enough. Master Heminge found me comfortable lodgings, sleeping in a room with Roger and the boys who were actor apprentices. I was given a pair of boots from the costume box and, to earn my keep, I spent my days sweeping floors or painting scenery or sorting costumes.

But one morning everything changed.

The actors were waiting to begin rehearsals for the next play *Twelfth Night* when Master Shakespeare came bursting into the theatre. He was usually even tempered, but that day something had made him very angry. 'Where are they?' he roared.

Master Burbage, who was our finest actor, was not pleased by this outburst. 'Where is who, Will?' he asked.

'The boys! The boys!' yelled Master Shakespeare. 'Where are they?'

Master Kemp came running over to him. 'Calm yourself, Will. We think they are still in their beds. We've sent Roger Burman back to the lodgings to wake them.' By then Master Shakespeare's face had turned purple with rage.

'Asleep? At this hour? No, no they are not. Mark my words.'

Master Kemp tried to calm him. 'What is it, Will? Are your teeth bothering you?'

'No. Not my teeth. I'm told that the apprentices have left us and gone to the city.'

'Left?'

'Gone! Have you not heard that Edward Pearce has set up a troupe of boy players at St Paul's?'

'Indeed I have not,' said Master Burbage. 'But what has that to do with us?'

'Richard, you are a fool,' snapped Master Shakespeare. 'Her Majesty has seen fit to allow boys to perform within the city whilst we must keep our playhouses outside.' He roared like a lion and paced backwards and forward. 'Is that fair? I ask you. Is that fair?'

'Sit down, Will,' Master Kemp insisted. 'All will be well.'

'No. All will not be well. We have no boy actors, and our audiences will not travel outside the walls while they can see the so-called Paul's Boys.'

He was in a terrible temper.

But it turned out to be true. The boys had gone. The landlord himself told Roger. They had run off to the city, he said, hoping to join Paul's Boys and earn better money.

Of course, all this trouble was a great piece of luck for me. As there were no boy actors to be had, both Roger and I were asked to take a part to which we readily agreed. Roger was to play a girl called Viola and I was to be a rich young countess called Olivia.

'You must prepare well for the parts,' Master Shakespeare insisted. 'You will need a great deal of training.'

We were immediately put in the charge of Master Burbage

who was to teach us acting skills. Although he was a strict master and worked us hard, he was a good teacher. We learned how to memorise our lines and remember our cues. We were taught how to move around the stage, when to stand still and how to speak out clearly.

'Every member of the audience must hear you,' he insisted. And he made us repeat our lines over and over until he was satisfied.

For days Roger and I worked long hours until Master Burbage considered us good enough to go before an audience. I was buzzing with excitement and didn't care that I was to be a girl with a frilly gown and itchy periwig.

I could hardly wait for the day of my first performance. But when it arrived I found that I was sick with fear. I stood at the side of the stage, quaking and shaking as the theatre filled with folk from the city. And by the time it was full and the play was about to begin, my heart was beating so fast that I thought it would burst from my chest.

It was a terrible feeling, but then something quite amazing happened. As soon as I stepped in front of the audience my fear vanished as if by magic. I spoke my lines. I strutted about the stage. I nodded and smiled with my head held high. And when I heard gasps and *oohs* and *ahhs* from the crowd I knew I had made the right choice. I was meant to be an actor indeed.

Weeks passed and I fitted easily into the life of the theatre. Then one morning we all gathered in the Curtain to discuss the next performance. Master Shakespeare arrived last of all to begin the discussion. Even after all these weeks I found it hard to look at him or speak to him without shaking. I could not believe that I was here in London with the man I most admired in the whole world and I often feared that I was dreaming and would soon wake up. He stood in front of us, holding a script in his hand. 'Our next play, gentlemen,' he said, 'is to be *Romeo and Juliet* for it is popular with our audiences.'

There were whispers around the room. Every actor was anxious to hear which part he would have – who would have the biggest role? Who would have the smallest?

Master Shakespeare paused and smiled directly at me, and I wondered if it eased his pain a little that I reminded him of his poor son, Hamnet.

That day he had good reason to smile at me. 'Master Burbage tells me you have done well, Thomas,' he said. 'I have seen for myself how quickly you have learned and what a good actor you are for one so young. I am proud of you.'

'Th-thank you, sir,' I stuttered, my cheeks flushing pink. I waited for him to speak again and, when he did, my mouth fell open in surprise.

'Both you and Roger have done very well and so you are to play the title roles.'

There were gasps all round. Master Burbage's apprentices were to play Romeo and Juliet! I felt like leaping to my feet, running up to the roof and shouting the news to the whole of London. But instead I replied in my best scholarly manner. 'I will do my best, sir.'

Then Roger spoke. 'Pardon me, sir. But which one am I to play? Romeo or Juliet?'

'You are taller than Thomas, Roger,' he replied, 'and so you will play Romeo. Thomas will play Juliet.'

I must admit, I was disappointed for I would have preferred to play Romeo. But I needed to be patient. I was growing fast and I would soon be too big to play the part of a girl.

In the days that followed, Roger and I rehearsed some scenes together and Master Burbage came to help us. There were a great many lines to learn but I worked hard, sometimes whispering them to myself at night as I fell asleep.

When I got my role in *Romeo and Juliet* I thought about Alice a lot, knowing how much she liked that play.

And then one day in October she came to watch.

It was after the performance, when we were packing away the props, that I spotted her standing by the door, waving to me. 'Thomas!' she called and came hurrying across the room. 'I didn't recognise you, I swear. Ain't you a sight dressed as Juliet!' And she clapped her hands to her cheeks and rocked with laughter.

That afternoon we walked across the field by the roadside and Alice bombarded me with questions about the theatre.

'Do they treat you well? Who is the finest actor in the troupe? Have you acted before the queen?'

And she wasn't satisfied until I had told her all.

'Well,' she said when I had finished. 'That's a fine life, ain't it, Thomas?'

'It is,' I replied. 'I always dreamed of working with Master Shakespeare.'

'Is he a kind old cove?'

'I've no complaints except that he suffers with his teeth and his breath stinks.'

'Poor soul. There is nothing so painful as rotten teeth.'

'But what about you, Alice? Did you find work?'

'I did,' she replied. 'But it weren't no better than serving at the tavern.'

'Why?'

She screwed up her face as if she had cracked a rotten egg. 'Well, first I was with the washerwomen by Moorfields, dragging the linen from the water and spreading it out to dry. I earned no more than a few pennies. I ask yer! So I went cleaning fish by Billingsgate. The pay ain't much better and it's horrible! Just look at me hands, Thomas.' She showed me her fingers which were cracked and red raw. 'It's freezing cold work and I stink of fish. Can you smell it on me?'

You could smell the fish at twenty paces but I thought it best to say nothing. 'Will you try to get other work?' I asked.

She looked at me and winked. 'I've found new work already.' We settled on a tree stump while she told me. 'Tomorrow, I take up my post with an apothecary in Cheapside.'

'An apothecary?'

'They mix potions and medicines. Don't you know that?'

'I know that,' I said. 'But why would an apothecary take on a girl apprentice? Surely only boys would do such work.'

She frowned and flapped her hands. 'Oh *poof*! There you go again, Thomas. A girl can't do this. A girl can't do that. Am I a freak? Can't I keep his workshop tidy? Can't I learn where each bottle is stored and when it needs filling?'

I laughed. 'Of course you can. But I have never heard of a girl working for an apothecary.'

She looked down at her lap and fiddled with her skirt. 'Well...' she said. 'The truth is nobody else wants to work for him.'

'Why so?'

'He's foreign, that's why. They're afraid just cos he don't speak like us and he has dark eyes and his beard is as black as coal.' She tossed her hair back from her face. 'I believe he comes from Spain, Thomas. But what's wrong with that, eh? Just because the whole of London is scared witless of Spaniards. 'Tis nonsense! I don't listen to such gossip.'

'Alice! Is this wise? What if the rumours are true? Spain would invade us if they could.'

'Oh fie!' she said throwing up her hands. 'He is a clever man with grand clients and he'll pay me three times what the fish market pays. I'll just take care of his cures and see to his herbs.' She laughed. 'His shop is close off Milk Street and it don't half smell lovely, Thomas. Ain't that better than fish, eh?'

'Are you sure about this, Alice?'

She folded her arms across her chest and lifted her chin. 'As sure as my name's Alice Trowte I shall be an apprentice to Master Gideon de Laine.'

I had an uneasy feeling in the pit of my stomach. 'He may be dangerous,' I said. But, if I'm honest, I couldn't blame her. I would have risked taking the job rather than work every day with stinking fish.

She stood up, ready to leave. 'I'll come back soon and tell you how I fare,' she said as we walked together towards Bishopsgate and there we parted company. Alice waved good-bye and went skipping away into the city, not knowing what the future held for her.

Chapter 18
Don't You Know Me?

In the weeks that followed, the weather grew colder. Master Shakespeare had received a summons from the queen to write a play for the Christmas festivities.

'One play!' he said, running his fingers through his hair. 'Last year it was two. This is not good news,' he said to Master Burbage. 'Can it be that she has invited the Admiral's Men to perform? Heaven help us. Are we not excellent players? Are my plays not better than theirs?'

'Stay calm, Will,' said Master Burbage. 'I believe the queen was well pleased with us.'

'She was not pleased with *Richard II*, remember.' He marched backwards and forward across the room, his temper growing worse by the minute. 'And what do I do about boy actors? Most of ours are gone and the players are having to take two parts or more. Things get worse and worse.'

Things didn't get any better when, one evening as we all sat eating supper at the White Hart, Master Shakespeare said quite suddenly, 'I'm afraid we must soon move from the Curtain.'

Most of us round the table looked shocked. Only Master Kemp and Master Burbage didn't look surprised. I expect they already knew about it.

'We have a quarrel with the landlord,' he continued. 'So I

have been looking for a site where we can build a new theatre. 'Tis a worry indeed for if I don't succeed we'll have nowhere to perform and we shall be wandering vagabonds. Be assured that I am doing my best.'

In addition to this problem Master Shakespeare was in a real pickle with his teeth, and he was often seen holding his head in his hands or rubbing his cheek. To ease the pain he would grab a handful of cloves and chew on them, which I think must have helped a little bit.

One day, in the middle of November, I had just finished another performance of *Romeo and Juliet* and was leaving the Curtain when I bumped into a lad waiting outside the door. I reeled back, only just managing to stay on my feet as the boy stood and stared at me.

'Don't you know me?'

'I don't think so,' I replied, for the boy looked pinched and rough as if he was the fighting sort. So I turned and walked away, not wanting any trouble.

'Thomas, stay,' he called after me.

At the sound of my name, I spun round and faced him. I stared, wondering if it could be somebody I knew. Behind the bruised cheeks there was something familiar. The eyes were blue and clear. The hair, cut close to the head, was a colour I knew well and in that moment I realised that this was no boy.

It was Alice.

I gasped at the sight of her. How changed she was! Her hair, which had been so thick and long, had been hacked off and now stood on her head in red tufts. Instead of a skirt, she wore breeches and hose and a leather jerkin. So you'll understand why I mistook her for a boy. But there was worse. One side of her face was swollen and blue with bruises as if she had been badly beaten.

'Alice!' I gasped. 'What's happened? And why are you dressed like this?'

She looked away, ashamed and miserable.

'Tell me,' I said, taking hold of her arm, which only made her wince with pain and she shrank away from me.

When she finally spoke it was quietly under her breath. 'I am a fool, Thomas. You were right. I should not have worked for the apothecary.'

'Why so, Alice?'

She shrugged her shoulders. 'His customers didn't like to see a girl in the shop. They said it wasn't right. So Master de Laine said I was to dress as a boy.'

'And you did?'

She raised her chin and looked at me. 'He said if I didn't he'd kick me out into the street, Thomas. He paid me well enough, see, and Ma was glad of the money to feed the boys.'

'Did your mother think it was right, you dressing as a lad?'

Alice turned away, lowering her eyes. 'She never knew what I was doing. Master de Laine gave me a set of boy's clothes which I kept in the shop. Every morning when I went to begin work, I changed into 'em and tucked my hair under a cap.'

I pointed at the bruise on her face. 'He hit you, didn't he?' I said. She nodded and touched her swollen cheek. 'Why?'

'I found out things about him.'

'What things?'

She hesitated. Then, as if she wanted to confess, the words poured out in a torrent. 'He makes poisons, Thomas. It's a terrible thing. If they wants somebody killed, they pay Master de Laine a fortune and he gives 'em one of his special potions.'

I stared at her. Had she lost her mind? 'That can't be true, Alice,' I said. 'Are you sure?'

She nodded. 'I suspected that some of the potions were dangerous – but now I know for sure. I've got proof.'

'What proof?'

She began to tremble as if she was too frightened to say more. But I led her down the road, away from the Curtain and made her sit on a low wall to rest. Then, bit by bit, she told me what she had found out.

'I work most of the day in the room above the shop where he keeps the bottles and herbs.' She was twisting her fingers nervously as she spoke. 'This morning, I was on the stairs carrying a potion down to Master de Laine when a gentleman came into the shop. I heard quite clearly what he said. I couldn't help it – I swear! I should have gone back upstairs, I know, but I didn't. Instead I peeped through the curtain at the bottom.' She shivered violently, remembering what she had seen, afraid to tell me more.

'Who did you see, Alice? Who was it? Do you know his name?'

She shook her head. 'But I knew he must be rich for he had a big belly and fine clothes. He had a servant with him.'

112

Here she paused before she could speak of him. 'He was a fearful, cruel-looking man, Thomas. He had a terrible scar running from his mouth up to his ear, and he had a crooked eye too.' She shivered at the thought of it.

'What happened then, Alice?'

'I saw the apothecary hand the gentleman a little glass bottle, and he said, "A drop on an earring will be sufficient." The gentleman smiled a wicked twisted smile and told Master de Laine that they had a pair of earrings ready. "Emeralds," he said. "A gift for Her Majesty at the Christmas festivities."'

'He mentioned the queen? Are you sure you heard it right, Alice?'

'I am sure, Thomas. He said it would be a present from Spain and they laughed as if it was a great joke. Then I heard the apothecary say, "Death will occur soon after it has touched her skin. You have my word." I heard him say it. Truly I did! I remember all of it.' Tears welled up and spilled onto Alice's cheeks as she looked at me.

'What happened then?'

She wiped away the tears and sniffed. 'The servant handed Master de Laine a bag of gold which he tipped out on the counter. Oh, I was so afraid, Thomas. I turned to go upstairs, but, in my haste, I tripped and fell.'

'So the apothecary heard you?'

Alice covered her face with her hands, nodding miserably. 'Master de Laine flung back the curtain and dragged me down the stairs by my foot. When the gentleman saw me, he was that furious he snatched hold of my ear. Then my cap fell off, see, and he could tell I was a girl. He went wild and yelled at me. "Have you been listening to our conversation, wench?" Then he slapped me across my face so hard that I cried out. Heaven help me! He dragged me across the counter, took hold of a pair of scissors and hacked off my hair while I screamed and screamed. Then the apothecary shut me up with his hand across my mouth and that servant set about me with a stick until I lost my senses.'

'Alice!' I gasped. 'Such terrible things! How did you escape?'

My friend paused and wiped her cheeks before she continued. 'They left me for dead on the floor but my ears were still sharp. I heard that evil apothecary say to the men that he would go to Ma's house and tell her I had died sudden of the fever so she wouldn't come looking for me.' Alice was choked with tears. 'Oh, Thomas, then the worst thing. That evil man said he would come back and get rid of my body after dark.'

Alice broke down, racked with sobbing. I was so shocked that I couldn't speak but waited for her to calm down and finish her story. 'I was in terrible pain. You can see the bruises on my face, can't you, Thomas? And my legs and back were beaten too.'

'Then how did you manage to get away?'

'Somehow I struggled to my feet and – merciful heaven – I found a hairpin on the floor among the heap of my hair. Pa showed me how to pick locks years ago, see, so that's what I did. I used the hairpin and opened the door.'

'And you came here.'

She gripped my hand. 'I daren't go home. That would be the first place the apothecary would look, see. But I knew I had to get out of the city. The old devil has his spies and they'd find me. So I thought of you, Thomas, and I came here as fast as I could. Those men are evil! Evil!'

'We should go and find a constable, Alice.'

But she shook her head wildly. 'It ain't no use, Thomas. Who would believe somebody like me?'

She was right. A girl dressed as a boy with her face swollen and her hair hacked off as if she had escaped from the asylum.

She looked up at me, pleading. 'What shall I do, Thomas? What shall I do?'

Chapter 19

Rotten Teeth

There was no doubt about it – I had to help Alice. Not long ago she had helped me get to London and had brought me safely to the Curtain. Without her I could well have got lost or succumbed to cut-throats, for London was a mean city. Now it was my turn to repay her.

'I have an idea, Alice,' I said, hoping to calm her. 'Master Shakespeare is still short of boy actors.'

She looked at me blankly.

'You are used to dressing up in boy's clothes, aren't you?'

She still didn't understand.

'Listen, Alice. You could join the Chamberlain's Men as a boy actor, like I did. Who will guess you're a girl, eh? You'll be safe with us and that devil apothecary won't find you.'

But the idea alarmed her. 'No, Thomas,' she said, leaping to her feet. ''Tis against the law for a girl to be on the stage. I will be found out. I will be put in prison. No, no, no!'

In the end, after a good deal of talking, she realised it was the only way. She had nowhere else to go. My plan was a dangerous one but she knew it was a risk she had to take. And so she agreed.

'And will you tell Master Shakespeare about the poison?'

I chewed on my bottom lip while I thought. 'I don't know,' I said eventually. 'Let's go to the Curtain and I'll think about it.'

She nodded wearily as if she was too tired to disagree.

'You will need a new name,' I said. 'What shall we call you?'

'Barnaby,' she said sadly. 'It was the name of my youngest brother taken by the plague.'

She plucked up her courage, wiped her cheeks, and together we walked up the road towards the Curtain. When we arrived Will Kemp and the rest of the troupe had just finished packing away after the performance.

'Ho, Thomas!' called Master Kemp, raising his hand as he saw us enter. 'I see you have brought a friend.'

'Barnaby, sir,' I replied as we walked towards him. 'He has come from the country and would like to join our troupe.'

He turned to Alice. 'Do you act, young sir?' he asked leaning forward, his hands clasped behind his back.

'A little,' Alice whispered.

'But I see from those bruises that you enjoy a fight.'

'Not much, sir,' she replied.

'Indeed!' he said, taking her chin between his thumb and forefinger and peering closely at her face. 'For all your bruises, you have a soft face. I think you would play the part of a maid very well, Barnaby. Now, show me how a lass would walk across the room.'

Alice hesitated but then set off for the far side while we watched.

'Excellent!' called Master Kemp, clapping his hands a she came back towards him. 'You can walk like a real girl. Well done, Barnaby.'

By then Master Burbage had joined us. 'What of your

117

speech, boy? Can you speak clearly? And can you speak as a maid?'

'I can, sir. I have as light a voice as any wench.'

Master Kemp looked at Alice. 'But what about lines, Barnaby? Can you learn them? Are you quick at your studies?'

My stomach knotted as I remembered that Alice could not read. 'Barnaby is well acquainted with Master Shakespeare's work, sir,' I interrupted. 'He can speak lines from *Romeo and Juliet*.'

Alice held up her chin, trying to look confident. 'Indeed I know them well, sir.' And she stepped away from Master Kemp and stared into space as if towards an audience and recited the same words she had spoken at the Black Boar.

'How if, when I am laid into the tomb,
I wake before my time that Romeo
Come to redeem me?'

It was well said and I felt proud of her. She had spoken the words better than any man.

'Well done! Well done indeed, Barnaby!' said Master Kemp. 'I shall be happy to take you on as an apprentice and teach you what I know.' He clapped his hands above his head to attract the attention of the actors. 'Leave your work, men,' he called. 'We have a new member of our troupe. Let us take Barnaby to the White Hart and welcome him as one of the Chamberlain's Men.'

So we all left the Curtain and walked down to the tavern, where we spent an hour or so toasting Alice with the landlord's best ale.

*

After such a warm welcome, Alice settled in well and recovered from her ordeal. She soon became her old chattering, bossy self and had no problem behaving like a real boy. She could spit and swear like the rest of us and no one guessed that she was a girl. She did jobs around the theatre and didn't even flinch when Roger Burman asked her to fill pigs' bladders with pigs' blood.

'Messy job, eh?' he said, nudging her with his elbow. 'The audience likes fight scenes, see. They love blood and gore, they do.'

All this time, I said nothing to Master Shakespeare about what Alice had seen and heard. I was too afraid. Master Kemp gave Alice acting lessons and she learned well. Master Shakespeare was so impressed with her that she soon had lines to speak on the stage.

'I have never seen a boy apprentice so convincing in the part of a girl,' he said. 'You are a wonder, Barnaby.'

And although Alice couldn't read, she had a most excellent memory. To help her, I would speak her lines out loud and, after repeating them only twice, she would remember them, word for word.

She had been with us for three weeks when one afternoon we were alone together in the tiring room. We were brushing the costumes ready for the next play when she suddenly said, 'It ain't right being here, Thomas. We ain't told nobody about that apothecary's poison and, worse, Ma thinks I'm dead. It ain't right, I tell you.'

I ignored her and took another shirt out of a large wooden box.

'Well, I decided I'm going to see Ma. As soon as the rehearsal's over. And that's that!'

'You can't go,' I said.

'I can,' she insisted, fixing me with those piercing blue eyes. 'Tell Master Burbage I'm sick or something. I won't be long. And I'll tell Ma what I heard in the shop. She'll know what to do.'

I was horrified. 'And what if Gideon de Laine or one of his rogues sees you in the city? You'll be done for.'

She clenched her fist and thumped it on the table. 'It's no good. I can't stand it no more. It ain't right, me being here when Ma thinks I'm dead.'

'But you've got to stay safe,' I protested. 'You can't put yourself in danger.'

We squabbled for some time. I gave her my reasons over and over until she finally said, 'Oh, if you say so,' and flounced off in a temper.

I thought I had won the argument but I should have known better. The following day, something happened which had terrible consequences.

We were going over our lines and practising our cues for *Much Ado About Nothing,* which was the new play for the queen. Master Shakespeare was standing by the wall listening to us when he suddenly slumped onto a bench, groaning and clutching his jaw.

'What is it?' called Master Burbage and hurried over to him.

'Heaven help me,' he cried. 'My head is screaming for relief. Even the cloves do nothing to stop the pain.'

Master Kemp came too. 'Will, 'tis time you had that tooth out. The pain will not stop until you do.'

'Keep your advice,' Master Shakespeare snapped back. 'I'll not go to one of those butchers.'

Master Kemp threw up his hands in despair. 'Then there is nothing to be done. You must put up with the pain.'

Master Shakespeare looked at him, miserable and frightened. 'But my tooth will be ripped out from its sockets,' he moaned. 'I shall be left bleeding and in worse pain than before.'

It was then that Alice stepped forward. 'I have heard of a man in the city who pulls teeth, sir,' she said. 'They say he works miracles.'

Master Shakespeare raised his eyebrows and stared at her. 'How do you know of such thing, Barnaby? You are from the country, are you not?'

She hesitated for a second and my heart stopped, fearing that she would give herself away.

'Er, I stayed in London for some time before I came to seek out Thomas,' she said. 'I know the streets well.'

Master Shakespeare's eyes suddenly filled with hope. He was like a drowning man who clutches at straws. 'Tell me, where is this miracle man?'

'Over near Walbrook. I can take you there, sir. It's not far.'

Oh cunning Alice! I knew at once what she had in mind, for Walbrook was not far from the Trowte family home. While Master Shakespeare was having his tooth pulled, she would slip over to visit her mother in spite of my warning. I couldn't let her do it.

I pushed her aside and stood between her and Master Shakespeare. 'Sir!' I said. 'Barnaby has scenery to paint – five trees and a seat. There are but six days before we perform the new play for the queen and there's much to be done.'

But Master Shakespeare flapped his hand at me. 'The scenery can wait, Thomas. I must have some relief.'

'Then let me take you, sir. I too know of this man. Barnaby can stay and finish his work.'

Alice gritted her teeth and glowered. I'm sure that if she had had a knife, she would have plunged it into my heart.

'In truth, I care not who takes me,' Master Shakespeare groaned as he held his head in his hands. 'I only ask that we go at once and find this man who will stop the pain.'

'I will fetch your cloak, sir,' I said. 'It is cold out.' I hurried through the door at the back of the room, beckoning Alice to follow me.

'How could you try such a trick?' I fumed when we were out of ear shot.

'And how can you be such an evil goat!' she snarled then kicked wildly at my legs and beat me with her fists until I managed to grab her arms and stop her.

She broke into angry sobs. 'I must get news to Ma somehow, Thomas,' she cried. 'No matter what you say, I can't let Ma believe I'm dead. I can't. I've been thinking about it ever since I came here.'

'You mustn't go, Alice. It's dangerous. Now tell me who this tooth puller is and where he lives.'

She sniffed away her tears and crossed her arms over her

chest defiantly. 'I ain't tellin' you nothin' unless you go and see Ma.'

I stood and thought about it. It would be easy enough to run to Wood Street while the tooth puller was doing his work. I could go and talk to Mother Trowte and be back before Master Shakespeare was ready to come back to the Curtain.

'Right,' I said. 'I'll do it.'

'Promise?'

'I promise.'

Alice breathed a great sigh of relief. 'The tooth puller's name is Joshua Grimbald and you'll find him in an alley off Walbrook,' she said.

'I am not sure I can find it,' I said. 'I'll fetch a piece of paper and write it down.'

With a pencil I drew a simple map as Alice gave me the directions. 'Second on the right. Then left. Tis no distance from Ma's house.'

And so the plan was hatched.

Chapter 20
The Pelican

A bitter wind and icy rain pelted our faces as Master Shakespeare and I set off to find the tooth puller. My poor master shuffled along with his head bent and his cloak pulled across his mouth to protect it from the cold. Even so, he groaned with pain as we headed through Bishopsgate and down Threadneedle Street.

I took out the little piece of paper and looked at the plan I had drawn on it. There was no fear that Master Shakespeare would notice for he could think of nothing but his pain.

'We're almost there, sir,' I said, trying to comfort him. 'Your tooth will soon be out.'

We hurried towards Walbrook, by which time we were soaking wet. But when we finally turned off the main street and into a narrow close, as Alice had directed, we found it badly flooded from the rainwater pouring off the roofs.

'Heaven preserve us, Thomas,' Master Shakespeare moaned as we sloshed our way ankle-deep in filthy ice-cold water. 'Are you sure we are in the right place?'

'I am, sir,' I said and pointed to a door not two paces away on which a sign was nailed:

DOCTOR JOSHUA GRIMBALD
OLD TEETH REMOVED.
NEW TEETH FIXED SECURELY IN PLACE.

'This is it,' I said and knocked. We waited for some time until the door was opened by a servant, scrawny and bent with age, who beckoned us to follow him down the gloomy hallway.

At the end, he pointed to a door on the right. 'Wait in there, kind sir,' he quaked and shuffled off to find his master.

The room into which we stepped was dark and dusty, and smelled of something that reminded me of rotting horse flesh. It was so unpleasant that I placed my hand across my nose to block it out. There was a thin covering of straw on the floor which I noticed was badly stained – though I did not care to think with what. The only furniture in the room was a chair set in the middle and a table in the corner. That table, though plain and square, made me quake to look at it for it was spread with metal pliers and pincers of every size and shape. Some were sharp and pointed but most were old and brown with rust. Each one of them was for the purpose of removing teeth.

When Master Shakespeare glanced across and saw the implements, he shut his eyes moaning, 'Dear Heaven, Thomas. Must he use such vicious tools?'

Then he sank into the chair, holding his jaw in his hands and groaning in despair until footsteps sounded down the hall and the smell of ale and unwashed clothes arrived some seconds before Joshua Grimbald himself walked into the room.

He was a small, skinny man, almost bald with a patch of thin, lank hair hanging behind each ear. 'Welcome, sir,' he said, his smile revealing a mouthful of unnatural, ill-matched teeth which wobbled as he spoke.

'Welcome!' he repeated and shook my master's hand so vigorously that he cried out.

'Ah!' said the tooth puller. 'I see you have need of a doctor.'

A doctor? I had never seen anyone look less like one. Grimbald's stinking clothes were stained and his fingernails were cracked and broken and black as coal.

He leaned over my master, pinning him in the chair, and seemed to take delight in his patient's misery. No doubt he had noticed the quality of Master Shakespeare's clothes and, thinking he was about to make a good deal of money, he smiled even wider than before.

'How can I be of help?' he asked.

My master grunted and pointed to his cheek.

The tooth puller grasped his jaw with his powerful fingers, forced his mouth open and peered inside, ignoring his cries of pain.

'There is nothing to do but remove the offending tooth,' he declared as he let go of the jaw. 'It is too far gone for a lead filling.'

'Then take it out,' groaned Master Shakespeare.

Joshua Grimbald nodded and eagerly rubbed his hands together. 'If you would like a fine false tooth to replace it, I have a plentiful supply of persons I can call on. I can assure you of a perfect match. For a half crown I can fix a good tooth into your mouth.'

By this time, Master Shakespeare was rolling his head from side to side and groaning, 'No new tooth! Take this one out! Out!'

126

Grimbald shrugged and fetched a blood-stained apron off a hook, wrapping it round his waist.

'Then let us begin,' he said and walked to the table. His hand hovered over the pincers for a few seconds before finally picking the biggest tool and holding it up for the patient to see.

'I shall use this to remove the tooth,' he said, stepping closer and waving it under Master Shakespeare's nose. 'It is called the Pelican. A fine tool indeed.' He stroked it affectionately like a baby's head before opening it up and snapping it shut with a terrifying crunch.

Master Shakespeare's face drained of colour, and my own stomach churned to think that a tooth would be ripped out with such a thing.

Seeing the effect it had had, Grimbald smiled. 'You are afraid of the pain?'

Master Shakespeare, who was trembling from head to toe, nodded.

'Do not be afraid, sir.' The tooth puller spoke soothingly whilst holding the Pelican in front of my master. 'I have a special drowsy syrup made to my own recipe. It will take the pain away, if you wish.'

'Where is it? Give it to me.'

Master Grimbald returned the pincers to the table and picked up a small glass bottle from a dusty shelf. 'It is here, sir,' he said, waving it tantalisingly close, 'if you have the money.' He paused. 'Shall we say a crown?'

This was an outrageous price but my master fetched out

his purse with shaking fingers and placed the money in Grimbald's hand.

'And another crown for the pulling of the tooth,' he said.

I gasped at his greed but my poor master was in such pain he could not argue. As soon as the payment was made, Grimbald held the bottle to Master Shakespeare's lips and tipped the liquid so quickly into his eager mouth that it made him cough and splutter and almost choke on it. It was no more than a minute after the final drop had passed his lips that his eyes grew heavy and began to close.

'There,' said Grimbald, smiling in satisfaction. 'The potion is strong, is it not, boy? Your master will be sound asleep for an hour or so. Will you stay and watch me extract the tooth? I am exceedingly skilled. Do you like the sight of blood, boy?'

'No, sir,' I replied.

Grimbald laughed. 'Sometimes it is difficult to stop the flow. Go and walk about the city and come back when the clock strikes the hour. By then the rotten tooth will be gone.'

I hurried from the room and out into the alley. In spite of the cold and wet I was glad to be away from that place with its pincers and pliers and blood-stained floor. But I hated leaving Master Shakespeare with such a man. What if he died? I thought. What if he bled to death? What if the drowsy syrup was a poison?

With these terrible fears hanging over me like a thunder cloud, I waded through the filthy water in the alley and headed towards Cheapside.

Chapter 21
Back from the Dead

I ran through the back lanes and was soon into Wood Street, which was busy with carts and carriages making their way along the muddy road. But once I'd turned off and found myself in a labyrinth of dark alleyways things became difficult. I tried to look at the piece of paper for some clue as to which way I should go, but I could scarcely see. I turned up one close and down another but nothing brought me to Mother Trowte's house. Time was ticking by. I began to panic for I had to return to the tooth puller before Master Shakespeare woke.

I was about to give up the search when I suddenly spotted a sign hanging at the corner of an alley. It was in the shape of a boot and I remembered I had seen it near to where Alice's family lived.

Glad to have found it at last, I turned the corner and raced between the tumbledown houses to the top of the close and hammered on the rotting door of Mother Trowte's home. Slowly it opened and a small boy peeped through the gap.

'Who are you?' He screwed up his face. 'What do you want?'

He was about nine years old with blue eyes and tufty red hair that was so matted you couldn't pull a comb through it. Without a doubt, he was one of Alice's brothers.

'I'm a friend of your sister's,' I told him.

'Ain't got no sister,' he snapped and went to slam the door in my face.

But I stopped it with my foot. 'You've got a sister called Alice and I have news of her. I need to talk to your mother.'

He turned away from me and shouted, 'Ma. There's a rogue here says he knows our Alice. I'll give him a thrashin' if you wants.'

I didn't wait for the reply. I pushed him aside and stepped into the gloomy room where Alice's mother was sitting in the chair, just as before. She didn't move until I went and stood up close, bending my knees so that she could see my face.

'Mother Trowte,' I said. 'I'm Thomas. Do you remember me? I came a few months ago.'

She lifted her head and peered at me through narrowed eyes. 'Don't know you,' she grunted.

'I was with Alice.'

The boy barged between me and his mother. 'Leave her alone. She ain't so well since our Alice died. And she don't see so good. We looks after her, don't we, Willum?'

A second boy came out of the shadows. He was probably seven and a smaller version of his brother. Only dirtier. With a runny nose and no shoes.

'Why's he here?' Willum asked. 'We don't want no trouble, do we, Ma?'

Alice's mother shuffled in her seat. 'What d'you want, lad?'

'I've got some good news,' I said. 'Alice is alive and well.'

The old lady struggled to sit up straight. 'You mean she

ain't dead?' She blinked and rubbed her eyes and then a toothless smile spread across her face. 'Well I never did! Fancy our Alice coming back from the grave. That's a miracle, that is!'

'A miracle, Ma!' said Jack.

'Magic!' said Willum.

'But she never was dead,' I explained. 'That man who came to see you, Gideon de Laine, he told you lies.'

Mother Trowte's mouth opened and she stared at me, 'Lies? Well I never! He brought her clothes, he did. We sold 'em, didn't we, Jack?'

'We got sixpence, Ma. We ate well that week.'

'Aye. We did an' all.'

'Well,' I repeated, 'she's definitely not dead.'

'That is good news in an' mistake,' said Mother Trowte. 'But where is she?'

Jack stood in front of me with his hands on his hips. 'What's she gone and done? Is she in trouble with the constable?'

'She's run off, ain't she?' said Willum.

They were all talking so much that I held up my hands for quiet. 'If you'll let me speak, I'll explain.'

As they fell silent, Mother Trowte turned towards me, and the boys perched on the edge of the table, their heads cocked to one side ready to listen. I told them about the apothecary and how Alice was beaten and had run away to hide with the Chamberlain's Men.

'Why didn't she come here?' asked Mother Trowte. 'I'd have looked after her, I would.'

131

'Gideon de Laine's a dangerous man,' I said. 'He knows where you live, Mother Trowte. If Alice came here, he'd soon find out. She thinks he's Spanish and plotting with a wealthy gentleman to poison the queen.'

Ma Trowte clapped her hands to her face. 'Oh my lawd! Poison the queen? What are we coming to?'

'They say that Philip of Spain has sent spies to England and they are all over the city.'

'There! I knew it!' she said, slapping her hand on her knee. 'I always said them foreigners will be the death of us. We're not safe in our beds since Francis Drake went to his Maker.'

Jack jumped off the table. 'I know where that apothecary has his shop!' he said. 'I'll do for him, I will. You see if I don't.' And he bunched his fists, punching the air as if he was shadow boxing.

'Yeah,' Willum agree. 'We'll do for 'im, won't we, Jack?'

Alice's mother sat rocking in her chair scratching her leg. 'I always knew them apothi-what's-its were in league with the Devil. Our Alice should never have got in with a bad lot like him. She should have stayed cleaning fish. It were a steady job. We ate well, an' all. As many fish heads as we wanted.'

'Alice was worried. She wanted you to know that she was safe,' I said.

'But when is she coming home? I don't like to think of her living with them actor rogues. It ain't proper.'

'She'll come home as soon as she can, Mother Trowte. But she'll be glad to know that you're all well.'

'Except me eyes and me feet,' said Ma. 'They're not so good.'

'But we looks after yer, don't we, Ma?' said Willum, scratching his neck to relieve the flea bites. 'We do, don't we?'

'I'm the oldest,' Jack snapped at his brother and gave him a quick swipe across the head. 'I do most of the looking after yer, don't I?'

Then a fight broke out with Willum dodging most of Jack's punches and both of them screaming and yelling.

But Mother Trowte thought it a joke. She roared with laughter revealing her only tooth, which luckily reminded me that I should hurry back to Joshua Grimbald.

'I must go now,' I said, turning towards the door. 'Alice will be pleased to have news of you.'

'You take care of my girl,' Ma Trowte called as I lifted the latch. 'You tell her to come back soon.'

And with that, I headed down the alley and into daylight, hoping my master was safe and his pain was over.

Chapter 22
The Danger of Drowsy Syrup

I ran to the tooth puller's house only to find Master Shakespeare still asleep in the chair. His eyes were closed; his mouth hung open, dribbling blood. His shirt which had been white was sodden with dark red stains.

Joshua Grimbald was wiping his tools on his grubby apron as I walked in. ''Tis done,' he said, looking across at me and smiling. 'He bled a lot, I must say. Look there.' He pointed to the floorboards. 'It will have to be mopped.'

The floor was of no interest to me when my master seemed more dead than alive. 'Will Master Shakespeare recover, sir?' I asked anxiously.

The tooth puller sniffed. 'He has a weak constitution, boy. Like many who take the drowsy syrup, he is not strong. His sleep is as deep as death.'

At the talk of death, my heart sank into my boots. 'Will he wake, sir?'

'If the good Lord spares him,' Grimbald said with a shrug as he returned some pliers to the table. 'But if he does not, it will cost a half crown to have his body taken away. I hope there is more money in his purse, boy.'

My blood ran cold at these words and I was near to fainting. I rested my hand on the chair to steady myself and that was when Master Shakespeare groaned softly and turned his head.

'Sir, sir, can you hear me?' I cried, leaning over and gently shaking his arm.

He groaned again and this time his eyes fluttered open.

'Thomas?' he said – though his cheeks were so swollen and his mouth so full of blood that it hardly sounded like my name.

Grimbald clapped his hands noisily and leaned over my master, beaming broadly. 'Another successful extraction!' he declared. 'Was it not done well, sir? And did not my drowsy syrup remove the pain?'

My master moaned and raised his hand as if to push him away.

'Come, sir. A swallow of ale will clear your mouth.' The tooth puller picked up a wooden mug from the table and held it to my master's lips, tipping it so that the ale dribbled down his chin, turning pink as it mixed with the blood.

Master Shakespeare struggled to get to his feet. 'Let us go, Thomas,' he muttered. Though he tried to stand he was so weak that his legs could hardly support him and he had to lean heavily on my shoulders.

'Wait! Do not leave so soon, sir,' Grimbald called as we stumbled to the door. 'You would do well to discuss new teeth. I fit only the best.'

But my master did not answer and we lurched down the hall and out into the street. He was in such a bad way that it took us most of the afternoon to cross the city. The day was bitterly cold and the cobbles slippery from the rain. Every now and then we had to rest to let him recover his breath.

When we passed through Bishopsgate and finally reached his lodgings Master Shakespeare fell exhausted onto the bed and closed his eyes.

I left him sleeping and hurried to the Curtain where rehearsals were almost over for the day. The first person I saw was Alice.

'Thomas!' she called and hurried across the room anxious to speak to me. 'Did you see my ma?'

I was not pleased with Alice. 'Is that all you care about?' I retorted. 'Your tooth puller was a charlatan. A butcher. Master Shakespeare almost died.'

Alice stood glaring at me, her hands on her hips. 'Master Grimbald ain't no charlatan. Ma told me he paid her good money for her teeth. He's very clever, he is. He makes the finest false teeth for the gentry.'

'No, Alice. He is not clever. He's dangerous. His drowsy syrup almost sent Master Shakespeare into a permanent sleep.'

She snorted. 'Master Shakespeare took the drowsy syrup, did he? Well, Ma didn't need it when she had her teeth pulled. Neither did Uncle Henry. But Master Shakespeare would rather sleep than feel a bit of pain, would he?' She folded her arms and turned away. 'Well, I ain't surprised.'

Before we could talk more, Master Kemp called me over. 'How is Master Shakespeare's toothache, Thomas? Is it fixed?'

'Yes, sir. But he's taken to his bed and it will be some time before he's recovered.'

He threw his hands up in despair then slapped them on his forehead. 'Ye gods!' he roared. 'As if we have not enough problems.'

'But we have already learned the play,' I said, trying to calm him down. 'We have six days left for rehearsals. All will be well.'

'I hope you are right,' groaned Master Kemp. 'If we are not ready, the queen will have us in the Tower.'

Chapter 23
A Christmas Treat

Master Shakespeare took two more days to recover from his ordeal and all that time we were practising in small groups until, on the third day, he was well enough to join us for a full rehearsal.

He stood in the middle of the room with a stick which he struck on the floor. *Bang, bang, bang.* 'Gentlemen!' he called. 'Let us begin the first act. We perform for the queen in three days' time. We have work to do.'

Much Ado About Nothing was an exceedingly long play but we managed to run through all five acts, ending with the wedding scene. When we had finished, Master Shakespeare smiled and clapped his hands. He seemed pleased enough with our performances – especially Alice as she was word perfect.

'You have done well,' he said as we jumped down from the stage and gathered around him. 'I've no doubt that Her Majesty will be content with our play and that she will reward us handsomely.'

A cheer rose up from our troupe and we slapped each other on the back, glad that our hard work had not been in vain. A purse of gold from the queen was well worth having.

We were even more pleased when Master Shakespeare told us that there would be no rehearsals the next day, which was Christmas Day.

More cheers.

'And as a reward for your hard work,' he said, 'we shall meet at the White Hart at midday and eat a hearty meal together.'

The next morning came cold and bright with a light fall of snow as we walked towards the inn. By the time we arrived, the White Hart was crowded with people making merry but the landlord had saved a long table especially for the Chamberlain's Men. We all settled down, shaking each other by the hand, wishing a happy Christmas and raising a cup of mulled ale.

The feast that followed was wonderful. First the landlord's wife carried in a fine goose and that was followed by a boar's head with a rosy red apple stuffed into its mouth. For those who did not care for goose or boar's head, there was delicious pigeon pie with thick gravy. As the meal progressed and lots of ale was drunk the Chamberlain's Men grew more and more raucous with their joke telling and their noisy laughter. Even before the meal was cleared away, the boisterous Master Kemp leaped onto the table.

'Here, gentlemen! I give you a dance!' he shouted and began to skip in between the dishes while a man in the far corner stood up with a violin in his hand and began to play a tune, which made Master Kemp dance even faster until everyone in the room was laughing and cheering and clapping in time to the music.

It was a splendid Christmas, although I missed my family and wished they were here with me.

When Master Kemp had finished prancing about and had

climbed down from the table, a serving wench walked in with a large wooden bowl. 'Look!' I said to Alice, 'Here come the hot chestnuts.'

She made no comment but turned away. I didn't understand. Alice had been laughing with the rest of us and now she had suddenly turned quiet and withdrawn.

I nudged her with my elbow. 'What is it?' I asked. 'Is something wrong?'

'I can't help it, Thomas,' she said. 'It ain't right being here on Christmas Day. I keeps thinking of Ma and the boys. They won't have much in the way of food – and look at this lot.' She nodded towards the leftovers on the table. 'I could easy take some of this goose to Cripplegate. Ma would be as happy as a dog with two tails.'

I shook my head. 'No. We've talked about this. You can't go into the city.'

I must have raised my voice when I spoke and Roger, who was sitting next to me, overheard.

'What's up with Barnaby?' he asked.

'Nothing.'

'Nothing? Then why can't he go into the city? Is he in trouble? Been thievin', has he?'

Alice leaned forward. 'No, I ain't been thievin'. I just wants to go to Cripplegate to see me ma. Is that too much to ask on Christmas Day?'

Roger raised his eyebrows in surprise. 'You got a ma in Cripplegate? First I've heard of it. Thought you was from the country.'

I grabbed hold of his arm. 'Not a word, Roger. But I'm telling you that Barnaby must not be seen in the city.'

He grinned. 'And who's to see him on a snowy Christmas Day, eh? The streets will be as quiet as the grave save for church bells. And if you're worried that you'll be spotted, well, you can borrow me cloak and wrap it across your face. Who'll know you then, eh?'

It was kind of Roger to offer the cloak which Master Shakespeare had given him not long ago when the weather turned cold. It was smarter than anything else he owned and he was exceedingly proud of it. As for Alice going into the city – I still thought that it was a foolish idea.

Of course she didn't care what I thought and, with Roger on her side, there was no stopping her. She was so determined to see her family, it would be like trying to halt a rampaging bull.

'You can come with me if you wants to, Thomas,' she said, back to her old bossy self, 'but I ain't stopping here.'

She stood up and – bold as you like – asked Master Kemp if she could take some leftovers. He waved his hand and smiled. 'Of course, Barnaby. Of course. Take what you will to those who are less fortunate than ourselves. You are a kind youth.'

And so, against my better judgment, I set off with Alice and headed for the city as the snow fell steadily and covered the ground.

Chapter 24

Willum's Secret

The city on that snowy Christmas Day was quiet. No bustling crowds. No street sellers. No carts and carriages. There were only poor folk huddled in doorways and a few rooting pigs sniffing for their dinner.

We hurried along the streets, our heads bent against the icy wind, and by the time we arrived at Alice's house we were chilled to the bone.

The door was bolted so Alice hammered with her fist and shouted, 'It's me, Ma! Let us in quick. It's freezing out here.'

It was Willum who opened the door a crack and squinted at us, trying to make out who we were. But we were covered in snow and quite unrecognisable.

'Don't know who they are, Ma,' he shouted over his shoulder. 'Shall I get rid of 'em?'

'Don't be stupid, Willum,' said Alice and called out again, 'It's me, Ma!' as she pushed past him into the house.

Mother Trowte was sitting close to the fire which was burning low in the grate and giving off little heat. A stub of a candle flickered on the table, casting shadows around the room, as she looked up and smiled her almost toothless smile.

'So you're back, girl! Come in! Come in!' the old lady said. 'Well, I must say, I'm glad to see you.'

When Alice unwrapped the cloak, Ma's eyebrows shot up in surprise to see her in doublet and hose. 'What's this? You going round dressed as a lad? You still in trouble, are yer?'

'Just keeping safe, Ma,' Alice replied. 'I've come to wish you happy Christmas and I've brought you some fine goose meat and a slice of pigeon pie.' And she put the parcel of food on the table.

'That's a feast and no mistake,' said Mother Trowte, rubbing her hands with pleasure before picking up the meat and tearing it off the bone with amazing speed. Willum joined in straight away, pushing pieces of pie into his mouth until his cheeks were bulging.

'Save some for Jack,' Alice protested. 'Where is he?'

Her mother shook her head and continued chewing. Only when the food was gone and her fingers licked clean did she explain. 'Our Jack's got a job,' she said, sinking back into her chair and wiping grease from her mouth. 'He's working as a pot boy at the Crown. Been there a day or two.'

'He's there now, is he?' Alice asked.

'He didn't come home last night, so I suppose he is,' said Ma Trowte. 'Anyway, tell me about all this trouble what your friend here said you were in.'

'He's called Thomas, Ma.'

'Right. Well, tell me what happened. What's all this about that apothi-what's-it?'

Alice perched on the table and told her mother everything. How the apothecary made poisons, how he sold them to rich people and how she came to lose her hair.

'I didn't like the look of him when he came here with your clothes,' said Ma Trowte, wagging her finger at Alice. 'He's one of them Spaniards what fought Sir Francis Drake. Armada they called it. Trying to invade, they was.'

'That was years ago, Ma,' said Alice.

'They're still trying, my girl. Anyway, that man told us a pack of lies, didn't he? Told us you was dead. *Humph!* I said he was a bad 'un. Didn't I, Willum?'

'You did, Ma,' Willum replied. 'You said he was a bad 'un.'

We stayed as long as we could. Alice didn't want to leave, but we had to go before it grew dark and the gates were locked.

'Give your old ma a hug, girl,' said Mother Trowte and Alice threw her arms around her.

'I'll be back as soon as I can, Ma,' she called over her shoulder as we left. Then, as she wrapped the cloak across her face, she wiped a tear from her eye.

We had scarcely reached the end of the close when Willum came running after us.

'What is it?' I asked as he tugged at my sleeve.

'Secret,' he whispered.

'What secret?' said Alice.

Willum looked terrified. 'It's our Jack. He said I mustn't tell. But I'm scared. It's not right.'

Alice bent down and held his hands. 'What's not right, Willum? Tell me.'

He began to sob but, when he calmed down, he explained what was bothering him. 'Jack told a lie. Ma thinks he's at the

Crown, but he ain't. He's gone to work for that man what hurt our Alice.'

Alice gasped, horrified by what Willum had said. She bent down, holding him by his shoulder. 'The apothecary? Why did he do that?'

'He kept saying, "That devil deserves to hang." Said he was going to look for something. Said it was a secret.'

Alice hugged Willum and sent him back home. 'Leave it to us,' she called as he ran up the close. 'It'll be all right. You'll see.'

After he'd gone, there was no stopping Alice. 'I'm going to find Jack,' she said and set off running.

But going to the apothecary's house was madness.

'Why won't you listen?' I shouted as I raced to catch her up. 'He'll see you. What are you thinking of?'

But Alice had a strong will. After all, what girl would have dared to throw ale over a customer at the Black Boar? Or steal from the landlord? Or go and work for an apothecary? Alice was not a girl to do the sensible thing. She would always do as she liked.

'I don't care what you say, Thomas Munmore. I ain't leaving Jack with that old devil. I'm going to find him and that's that.'

The snow was no longer falling but the roads already had a thick covering as Alice marched on, leaving me scuttling after her and fretting that the gates would soon be closed and we wouldn't get back to our lodgings.

We had reached Milk Street when she turned into a narrow

close leading off to the side. 'It's down there!' she called. 'That's where he lives. Come on.'

The alleyway was dark with tall buildings on both sides. The upper storeys of the houses hung over, almost touching each other and the roofs were dripping with melting snow.

We walked through the slush, keeping under the shadow of the overhang so we would not be seen. Halfway down Alice stopped opposite a shop with a notice on the door which read:

MASTER GIDEON DE LAINE
WORLD FAMOUS APOTHECARY
TO THE GENTRY

We looked for some sign of Jack but the shop was in darkness. There was no sound. No movement inside. No Jack.

'Now what?' I whispered.

Alice gave a sigh and shrugged but didn't seem to have a plan.

I groaned and shuffled my freezing feet. 'So we've come for nothing, have we?'

She dug me in the ribs. 'Not so loud,' she whispered. 'Jack is in there. I'm sure of it.'

'Can you see through walls, Alice?' I snapped. 'Are you a magician?'

Before we could continue the argument, the upstairs room suddenly glowed with the flame of a candle.

'Look up there,' she said, pointing at the window. 'That's

the room where the old devil mixes his potions.'

'He must be working.'

Then, while we stood and watched, a shadow flickered across the window.

'It's the apothecary,' I said.

Alice gripped my arm. 'No!' she hissed. 'That shadow's too small. It's not him. It must be Jack.'

Like a dog sniffing a rabbit, she dropped down onto her knees and started scrabbling in the snow.

'Are you mad, Alice? What are you doing?'

'Finding a pebble. I'll chuck it at the window and he'll hear.'

'No! Stop! If the apothecary hears he'll come out and find us.'

But she already had a stone in her hand. Before I could stop her, she pitched it at the upstairs window and I covered my eyes, not daring to look.

The first pebble fell short. Then she tried again with a bigger one. There was a *clunk* and a *chink* as it struck its target. I held my breath and peeped through my fingers. The shadow was coming towards the window. Someone fiddled with the catch and flung it open. Then a head appeared over the sill and looked down at us.

'It's Jack!' squealed Alice. And then she called, 'Jack, we're here!' She jumped and waved her arms in the air as though she was trying to reach him.

Jack called down, grinning at Alice. 'Ho, sister! How did you know I was here?'

'Willum told us.'

'The old goat locked me in cos he don't trust me no more.'

'Is he in now?'

'No. But he'll be back soon.'

'Don't worry,' said Alice. 'We'll get you out of there.'

'How will you do that?'

'I'll think of something.'

'If I jumps, I'll break me neck.'

I left them arguing while I hurried down the close. I stood on the corner, keeping an eye open for the apothecary.

I looked in one direction and then the other, not knowing which way he would come. Milk Street was almost deserted and after five minutes or so, I saw someone approaching from Cheapside. It was a tall man with a long beard and a black robe flapping like crows wings. I had never seen Gideon de Laine but I guessed that this was him.

I turned and ran back to Alice. 'Quick! He's coming. Get inside, Jack, and shut the window. Alice, come on! We've got to hide.'

We hurried up the close, a few yards past the apothecary's door and stopped. Keeping our backs pressed against the wall, we stayed hidden in the shadows, waiting until we saw the apothecary come striding round the corner.

Alice grabbed my arm. 'That's him, all right,' she whispered.

As the villain came nearer, my heart beat faster. He seemed even taller now – like a bony giant who wandered the town scaring little children in their beds. Now that he was close, I could see that his robe was lined with fur like a wealthy man's. The sale of poisons must pay very well, I thought.

Alice and I watched, clinging onto each other, not daring to breathe. When he stopped outside his shop, he glanced about him before producing a large bunch of keys, unlocking the door and stepping inside.

'Let's go,' I said.

'What about Jack?'

'*Shh!*'

I took hold of Alice's arm and tugged her protesting all the way down the close and into Milk Street.

'I ain't going to leave him there,' she said twisting out of my grasp.

'Be sensible, Alice. He doesn't seem to be in any danger.'

She turned and glowered. 'How can you say that? He's locked up, ain't he? We've got to get him out and there's an end to it.'

'We can't do it by ourselves. We'll go back to the Curtain, think of a plan and get some help.'

But Alice was boiling with rage. 'You go, Thomas Munmore, but I ain't leaving our Jack with that poisoner.'

'Staying here all night isn't going to do any good. We've got to make a proper plan and come back tomorrow.'

'No,' she said, stamping her foot. 'Not tomorrow. We'll go back to Ma's house, that's what. We'll tell her what going on. She'll know what to do.'

I sighed and wondered how the old woman could possibly help. What could she do that we could not? But Alice insisted.

When we knocked on Mother Trowte's door, Willum

opened it. 'Why've you come back?' he whispered. 'Ain't you found our Jack?'

Without giving him an explanation, we stepped inside and found Mother Trowte, wrapped in an old shawl, sound asleep. Alice walked over, kissed her on the forehead and waited for her to open her eyes.

'Back so soon, girl?' Ma asked, scratching her neck. 'They've not locked the gates, have they? You can sleep here if you likes.'

Alice shook her head. 'It's Jack,' she said.

'Jack ain't back from his work yet. I told you.'

'He ain't at work, Ma. That apothecary's done for him. The one that done for me. Got him trapped in his house.'

Her mother swung round in her chair. 'What you talking about, girl?' she said, frowning and rubbing her hand across her chin. 'Jack's working as a pot boy at the Crown.'

'No, Ma. He's working for that apothecary.'

'Is he?'

'He is.'

'Little liar!' growled the old woman. 'He never said nothing about no apothi-what's-it.'

'He was trying to fix him, Ma. After the way he treated me,' said Alice. 'We don't know what to do next. That man's wicked. We've got to get our Jack out of there, Ma. Quick!'

'Gawd!' said Mother Trowte, poking her ear hole with her little finger. 'You young 'uns ain't nothing but trouble. I'd like a bit of peace and quiet – and what do I get? Trouble. Nothin' but trouble.'

'But can you help us, Ma?'

'Of course I'll help you, girl. We can't have our Jack mixed up with that devil, can we?' She gripped the arms of the chair and stood up. 'Willum,' she said. 'Go up and fetch the box. You know the one I mean.'

'You mean the one under the fl—'

'That's the one, son. Hurry now. Good lad.'

Willum disappeared up the ladder and soon returned with a wooden box under his arm which he gave to his mother. With a key from the mantelpiece she turned the lock and opened the box. Inside was a small leather bag, she shook it and five gold coins, stamped with flying angels, dropped onto her lap.

'Ma!' Alice gasped. 'That's a fortune! Where did you…?'

'Savings for emergencies. Nathanial and Nicholas gave 'em to me before they went sailing off to fight them Spanish.' She tapped the side of her nose and chuckled. 'Not sure where my boys got 'em.' She leaned forward and whispered, 'Ask no questions, that's what I say. The money'll come in handy now – for I've got a plan, my girl.'

Chapter 25

A Cure for Willum

To carry out Ma's plan, we had to return to the apothecary's shop. By then it was dark, and the temperature had dropped so much that the snow was crisp underfoot and sparkled in the light of a full moon. The four of us walked slowly down the road, for Mother Trowte's bunions were giving her terrible trouble and she had to take her time.

When we finally turned the corner into Milk Street, Alice called, 'It ain't far now, Ma. Nearly there.'

'Right you are, girl,' she replied as she hobbled behind. 'Now, you two make yourselves scarce. Leave the old rogue to me and Willum.' That was part of the plan.

Once we were in the close and near to Gideon de Laine's shop, Alice and I hid in the shadows while Mother Trowte limped through the snow to the apothecary's door.

Knock, knock, knock.

The sound echoed inside but no one came.

The old woman dipped her hand into her pocket and pulled out a short stick with a rounded knob on the end.

She banged it on the door. *Knock, knock, knock.*

Again no one came.

By this time Ma Trowte was in a real temper. She raised the stick and brought it with a wallop on the door, again and again and again, making a noise fit to wake the dead. People in the close threw open their windows. 'Oi!' they called. 'What's goin' on? Don't you know it's Christmas Day?' In spite of their complaints, she went on knocking until the apothecary finally unbolted the door.

'Cease your noise, woman!' he shouted, clutching his robe across his chest. 'Go away. My shop is closed for the night.' And he stepped back to slam the door shut. But Mother Trowte jammed the stick into the hinge. 'You remember me, sir?' she said in a voice quaking like an old crone. 'My poor Alice died in your service not long since, sir. You came to my house and brought her clothes. Very kind you were, sir. Very thoughtful.'

He hesitated as he registered who she was. 'Er, yes,' he said, clearing his throat. 'I remember. Are you begging? If so...'

'No, sir. I may be poor but I am too proud to beg. My boy is sick and I have heard of your potions and cures.'

'Does the child have the plague?' he asked, stepping back for fear of catching the disease. 'Is there swelling in his armpits or legs? Does he cough up blood from his lungs?'

'Nay, sir,' Mother Trowte assured him. ''Tis not the plague. He has the stomach sickness and vomits. Look at him, sir.' She nodded towards Willum who was standing a distance away, his head cast down and his shoulders drooping. 'He's like to fall on the ground, he is. Can you save him, sir?'

The apothecary pulled a kerchief from his pocket and covered his nose before reluctantly stepping a little closer to Willum.

'He has a sickness for certain,' he said, looking the small

153

boy up and down. 'But my potions are not free. Do you have money, old woman?'

'I have gold, sir,' she said. The apothecary raised his eyebrows in surprise and lowered the kerchief.

'I have some gold angels saved for me old age,' she continued, pulling out the little bag. 'But I will gladly give them for the life of my boy.' Then she poured the coins into her hand and held them out for him to see.

At the sight of the gold pieces, de Laine's expression changed from surprise to greed. 'For the sake of your daughter, Alice, I will make him a brew,' he said and reached out, eager for the money. But Mother Trowte was too quick and clamped her fingers over the coins before he could take them.

'Fetch me the medicine, sir, then the angels shall be yours.'

He looked at her and frowned. 'Very well,' he said, tucking the kerchief in his pocket. 'Wait here.'

'But, sir, cannot we come in? Tis bitterly cold and the child is sick.'

Gideon de Laine held up his hand. 'The fresh air will do him good. I shall go and mix a cure in my workshop.'

With that he disappeared inside, shutting the door behind him. Alice's mother pulled her shawl tight around her shoulders and sat on the step with her head in her hands, dozing. We stood in the shadows waiting for the apothecary to return.

Soon after the church clock struck seven, the door opened and Gideon de Laine marched out with a small glass bottle in his hand. But in the darkness, he failed to see Mother Trowte on the step and tripped over her. Then he went slipping and sliding in the snow, trying to keep his balance without dropping the potion and making a terrible noise as he did.

Alice's mother watched in surprise. 'Be careful, sir,' she called. 'Don't want you hurting yourself, do we?'

He managed to steady himself with the bottle still intact. But his face was black with fury, and I'm sure he would have marched back inside but for the thought of the gold coins.

'Where is the boy?' he demanded, glancing up and down the close. 'Is he not with you?'

'Oh, dearie me!' said Mother Trowte, struggling to get up off the step. 'Give me a hand, will you, sir? I'll find him. My poor knees are not as good as they were.'

The apothecary stepped away, clearly reluctant to touch her. Somehow she managed to heave herself into a standing position.

'Oh, lawd! Has my baby gone? Well, I'm blowed!' Then she called, 'Willum! Where are you, son?'

This went on for some time until a voice as weak as water called out from the far end of the close. 'I'm here, Ma.'

Mother Trowte tottered over to the apothecary. 'I don't see so well, sir,' she said, laying her hand on his arm. 'But I think he's not far away.'

He brushed her hand aside, fearful of infection, and moved in the direction of the voice. And this was our signal. Once he was a distance from the open door, Alice and I slipped inside the shop and ran up the stairs to the workshop. We turned the bunch of keys hanging in the lock and flung open the door.

'About time too,' said Jack as we burst in. 'What's taken you this long, eh? You've been messing about, ain't yer? Why haven't yer—?'

Alice covered his mouth with her hand to shut him up while I grabbed him by the arm and dragged him down the stairs.

Outside, some way away, Willum was having a noisy fit. Alice's mother was screaming, 'You've poisoned 'im! Oh, my good Lord! Oh, Heaven help him!' While all this was going on, the three of us were hurrying away unnoticed.

'Just look what you done!' Mother Trowte screeched at the top of her voice. 'My little boy is near to death.'

'But madam...' protested the apothecary.

'No! No! Do not touch him,' the old lady bellowed and clocked him on the head with her stick. 'Your medicines are evil. EVIL!'

'You vile old crone!' Gideon de Laine yelled back as he rubbed his head. 'My potion has not caused the fit.'

The two of them made such a terrible racket that neighbours flung open their windows again and bawled complaints which only added to the din. All this time we stood waiting in Milk Street. Then the shouting suddenly stopped. Doors and windows slammed shut and Alice's mother staggered round the corner with Willum in her arms.

'Oh, Heavens,' she gasped as she let the boy slide onto the snow while she flopped against the wall, panting heavily from the exertion – unlike Willum who immediately sprang back to life with a wide grin on his face.

'Did I do well, Alice?' he asked.

'You did brilliant,' she said and hurried over to her mother who was still panting and clasping her chest. 'You all right, Ma?' She put her arm around her. 'Just rest for a minute. You did well.'

Mother Trowte nodded, and once she had recovered her breath, she stood up and patted her hair. 'I'm right as rain now, girl,' she replied before turning to Jack and giving him a vigorous swipe with the back of her hand. 'This is your fault, my lad. Don't go telling me no more lies. Do you hear? And don't go getting mixed up with people you shouldn't.'

'Sorry, Ma,' said Jack, ducking away from another blow.

Mother Trowte tugged her shawl around shoulders and smoothed her skirt. 'Right,' she said. 'Now let's move sharpish.'

'Yeah,' Jack agreed. 'I'll be glad to get home.'

His mother spun round. 'What you thinking of? Ain't you been in enough trouble, Jack Trowte? Use your brains. We can't go home.'

'Why not?'

'Don't you know nothin'?' she said, prodding his chest with a bony finger. 'As soon as that old goat finds you gone, he'll send the Watch round – or some other rogue. He knows I'm Alice's ma, don't he? He knows where we live, don't he?'

'Then where are we going?'

'Your aunt Susan lives the other side of town. She'll have to put us up for the night.'

Chapter 26
More Money Than You'll Ever Have

We trudged through the snow across the city to Pudding Lane where Aunt Susan lived above the baker's shop. By the time we arrived, Mother Trowte's nose had turned scarlet and the boys had white rivers of snot running over their top lips. We were all frozen stiff in that bitter night and were not made any warmer by Aunt Susan's frosty welcome. When she opened the door to our knocking, we saw that she was ready for bed, night cap and all.

At the sight of us, her face creased into a frown. 'What is to do, sister?' she said. 'Why are you here bothering us on Christmas night? My husband is already asleep and must not be wakened.'

'No matter,' said Mother Trowte, pushing past her and beckoning us to follow her into the baker's shop. She looked around, wiping the drips from her nose, until she found a chair behind the counter and made herself comfortable. 'Let your husband sleep if he must,' she replied, waving her hand. 'But we all need a bed for the night.'

Aunt Susan's eyes grew wide. 'A bed? But there is no room, sister. Where shall you sleep?'

'By your warm ovens, girl. That will do very nicely... or will you turn your own sister out into the snow?' She sniffed. 'Your sister what looked after you when you was but an orphan babe. Your sister what fed you and clothed you like a mother.' Ma Trowte fixed the baker's wife with her beady eyes. 'So what's it to be?'

Aunt Susan shifted nervously. 'The ovens are cold. They were damped down hours ago. If we left them burning, we could set the whole town on fire.'

'Then we shall stay here,' Mother Trowte replied. 'Find some empty flour sacks and the children will make themselves beds as best they can. And bring us some bread, if you please.'

Once she had left us Ma chortled and winked at us. 'Since marrying Master Farriner, my sister has risen above her station. Her husband has fine plans. He hopes to be blessed with a long line of bakers so that the name Farriner will always be remembered.' Then she threw her head back, laughing. 'Who will remember Farriner, eh? Tell me that!'

Aunt Susan, who was fearful of her older sister, grudgingly returned with a loaf. Once Ma had eaten, it wasn't long before she dozed off in the chair, her mouth gaping open and snoring fit to frighten rats out of their holes.

The rest of us arranged the flour sacks on the floor and sat cross-legged in a circle. 'Tell us what happened at the apothecary's, Jack,' I said, chewing on the bread. 'Why did he lock you in?'

Jack shrugged. 'The old goat caught me snooping in his bedchamber...I thought he had gone out for a while but he came back unexpected and caught me. There's this chest over by the window, see. I'd looked in it before and I knew that black book was in there.'

'Which black book?'

'The black book with all his accounts in it. He writes down who he sells his potions to – I've seen him do it. I had to get it, didn't I?'

'You ain't half clever, Jack,' said Alice. 'Reading his book like that.'

'I went to petty school, didn't I?' her brother said. 'I'm a quick learner, I am.'

Alice grinned. 'He is, Thomas. He can read, you know.'

'Well,' continued Jack, 'when he caught me looking in the chest he thought I was looking for money, didn't he?' Jack laughed and tore a crust off the loaf, stuffing it in his mouth for he hadn't eaten all day. 'He was hoppin' mad, I tell you. He shouted at me, and then he kicked me like a dog.'

'He didn't hurt you, did he?' asked Alice, clenching her fists. 'If he did I'll . . .'

'Nah. He knocked me about a bit – but nothing much. He dragged me back to that room where he mixes his potions and he locked me in. Said I had to stay there – no food, no nothing. But I weren't scared.'

'Right,' she said. 'Then give us a peek at that book.'

I stood up. 'Let's move the candle nearer so I can read it.'

'Don't bother,' said Jack shaking his head. 'I told yer, he came back early.'

Alice stared at him. 'What do you mean, "He came back early"? You got the book, didn't you?'

He shrugged. 'How could I? I was locked in.'

Alice groaned and flopped dramatically onto the floor before pulling a sack over her head.

'Don't you go makin' a fuss, girl,' said Jack. 'I ain't got the book and that's a fact.'

More groans from Alice.

Jack tapped his forehead and winked at me. 'But I did read it, didn't I?' he continued. 'That day when I found it in the chest, I read his accounts and everythink.'

Alice flung back the sack and sat up. 'And?'

'Well,' said Jack, 'I got a good memory, I have. So I remember who the old devil sold the poison to.'

'Are you sure?'

'Course I am. Every day he made a note of what his customers paid him. A few pennies here for potions. A few pennies there for cures and herbs and that. But one date was different.'

'Which one?'

'The entry for the twenty-fourth of November.'

'November?' said Alice. 'That was when I was working for him.'

'Right,' said Jack. 'Well, on that day he wrote, *Special potion for Sir Walter Loddington.*'

'That doesn't prove anything,' said Alice.

'I think it does,' Jack insisted, leaning forward to add drama to his story. 'Whoever bought his special potion paid a very special price. The old goat wrote it in the book and it were more than a few pennies, I can tell you.'

'How much?'

'More money than you'll ever have in your life, girl,' he said. 'It were twenty gold sovereigns.'

Chapter 27

Fear of the Tower

We woke up the next morning to the smell of baking bread. Master Farriner must have been awake for hours and had already stoked the ovens and prepared the dough, yet we slept so deeply that we did not hear him.

He was not pleased to find us in his shop. 'Get up!' he bellowed and prodded each of us in turn with his foot. 'Get yourselves out of here before my customers come. Tis nearly daylight.'

The four of us who were sprawled out on the floor sat up at once, rubbing our eyes and stretching the stiffness out of our backs. Only Mother Trowte remained fast asleep in the chair, snoring softly with a regular rhythm.

The baker, a tall man with a big belly and bulbous nose, stood over us. 'I won't ask why you're sleeping in my shop,' he said, wiping his floury hands on his apron. 'You flea-ridden Trowtes are forever in trouble.'

On hearing these words, Alice's mother opened her eyes and sat up bolt upright, pushing her hair away from her face. 'I don't know what you mean, Master Farriner, I'm sure. We're a respectickle family, we are.'

But the baker ignored her. 'Clear up this mess and go. I'm not having the constable coming round. Bad for business.'

Jack looked up at him. 'Don't suppose we can have some bread, can we?'

'It's in the oven,' Master Farriner snapped, 'and you'll be long gone before it is ready for eating. So hop it.'

We helped Mother Trowte to her feet, folded the flour sacks and walked to the door.

'And don't come back!' the baker shouted as he slammed the door after us.

We stumbled along Gracechurch Street still half asleep. The icy wind from yesterday had dropped and the covering of snow had turned to a wet, grey slush.

Mother Trowte hung onto Alice and me for support owing to her bunions which had turned a terrible shade of purple in the cold. 'Where are we going?' she asked.

The only place I could think of was the Curtain. But what would Master Shakespeare say? He had welcomed me and later he had welcomed Alice too. But how would he feel about a strange woman and two grubby urchins?

'I'm sure Master Shakespeare will welcome you,' I lied, crossing my fingers behind my back. 'But just remember, Jack and Willum, they think your sister is a boy. Don't give the game away or we'll be in trouble. You must call her Barnaby.'

They glanced at each other and burst out laughing. 'Alice is a boy! Alice is a boy!' they sang as they raced round her, yelling and pulling faces until she lashed out at them and they darted away.

Our progress up the road to Bishopsgate was slow, and by the time we arrived at the Curtain, the final rehearsal for the new play had already started and Master Shakespeare was there to oversee it.

I had hardly stepped through the door when he spun round and shouted, 'Where have you been, Thomas? And where is Barnaby? He should be here.' He slapped his copy of the play against his thigh in irritation. 'This is our last rehearsal. You know well enough that we perform for the queen tomorrow.'

Just then Alice slipped in behind me with Jack and Willum, ragged and dirty, hanging onto her sleeves.

Master Shakespeare's eyes grew wide. 'And who are these?' he demanded, pointing at the boys. 'They cling to you like limpets, Barnaby. Are they beggars you have picked up from the streets? Do you think this is an almshouse?'

Before she could answer, the last of our group – Mother Trowte – arrived. She must have seemed a strange figure, with her straggly hair and her black tattered shawl, lurching unsteadily into the room and grasping hold of the doorframe for support.

Master Shakespeare's mouth fell open at the sight of her and his face flushed red. 'Heaven preserve us!' he cried, flinging the pages to the floor. 'Are we expecting the whole of London?' Then, shaking with rage, he glared at me. 'Who are these people, Thomas? Why have you brought them here?'

I could hardly get my words out for I was afraid of the great man's anger.

Instead, Alice answered for me. 'They are my brothers, sir,' she explained and, though she sounded bold, I could see her hands were shaking.

When I recovered my nerves I said, 'You are still short of boys, sir. Could those two join the Chamberlain's Men as apprentices? Barnaby is a good actor and I think his brothers will soon learn.'

'Maybe so,' Master Shakespeare snapped. 'But this is not the time. We perform for the queen tomorrow.' Then he glared at Mother Trowte. 'And who is this woman? Is she to be an apprentice?'

There were sniggers from the actors standing around the room.

Alice pulled herself up to her full height. 'She is my mother, sir,' she said with her chin held high. 'She can be useful to us. She can fetch beer from the ale house and mend the costumes.'

I wondered how Alice could lie so boldly. Mother Trowte would find it difficult to carry the beer any distance, and as for sewing – well, she could scarcely see the cloth.

Mother Trowte smiled a toothless smile in an attempt to be friendly. 'Yes indeed, sir,' she said. 'I can do the things that Alice spoke of.'

At the sound of that name my heart stopped and my blood turned to ice. Why had she called her Alice instead of Barnaby? Had she forgotten? I could see that Master Shakespeare was taken aback, confused.

He walked over to Mother Trowte. 'Am I going mad?' he said, speaking slowly as if she was hard of hearing. 'Who is this Alice you speak of? I see no Alice here.'

The old woman, realising that she had made a terrible

165

mistake, hunched her shoulders and slapped her hand across her mouth.

But Alice came to the rescue. She tossed her head back and laughed. 'Why, sir, my family call me Alice because my face is so much like a girl's. It is but a jest.'

Master Shakespeare relaxed and turned to Will Kemp. 'For a moment,' he said, wiping his forehead with his kerchief, 'I thought our Barnaby really was a girl. In truth, I feared that we were in serious trouble.'

'Aye,' said Will Kemp. 'Barnaby acts well. I should hate us to lose him so close to the performance at the palace.'

Master Shakespeare turned back to Alice, smiling. 'So they call you by a girl's name, do they, Barnaby? Does your family try to make of fool of you?' Then he grinned and punched Alice on the shoulder.

But Willum, not realising it was a playful gesture, let out a cry and ran forward to protect her.

'You stop that, you villain!' he shouted, trying to push Master Shakespeare away. 'You leave my sister alone. Just because she's wearing boys' clothes, don't think you can beat her up.'

A deathly silence fell upon the room. No one dared speak. Master Shakespeare's eyes flashed with anger as he glowered at the quaking Alice. All was lost, I knew it. We could not lie our way out of this.

'A girl?' he growled and moved towards her, pushing Willum aside. 'You...are...a...girl?' He said each word slowly.

Alice, terrified, sank to her knees in front of him while

166

Willum ran howling to Mother Trowte and clung to her skirt, not knowing what was going on.

Master Shakespeare grasped Alice's chin and lifted it so that she had no choice but to look at him. 'Do you dare to put us all in danger?' he demanded.

She couldn't speak.

'Did you not think what this could mean for the Chamberlain's Men?' he roared, flinging her away as if he could not bear to look at her. 'Because of you,' he said, spitting out the words with venom, 'these men might soon be languishing in the cells of Newgate. Because of you...'

'Please, sir,' she sobbed, 'I did not mean to. But you must help us. Please help us.'

He looked round at the actors. 'Out!' he barked. 'Out! Out! And mention this to no one – or suffer the consequences.'

As they scurried from the room, he caught hold of Master Kemp's arm. 'Stay with me, Will,' he insisted. 'We shall listen to what they have to say.'

Now the game was up. The truth was out. Master Shakespeare, with Master Kemp at his side, confronted me, his face black as thunder and those eyes of his looking so reproachful. 'You of all people, Thomas. You must have known this all along,' he said. 'I expected better of you. After all I've done for you.'

He looked away as if unable to face me. I was mortified. I hadn't wanted to deceive him. I only wanted to help Alice. I hung my head in shame and wished things could have been different.

Then he turned towards me again. 'I want no more lies,' he said. 'Tell me what is going on, Thomas. The truth!'

So I began at the beginning: how I met Alice at the inn on my way to London. And how she found work with an apothecary and how she saw him selling a poisonous potion and believed he was plotting to murder the queen. As he listened, Master Shakespeare raised his hand to his mouth horrified to hear such things.

Then Jack stepped forward and nudged my master. 'It was me what found out about the poison,' he boasted. 'I found this book, see. The old devil wrote everything down in it. The man what bought the poison was a right rich cove. He paid twenty gold sovereigns, he did.'

'What was his name?'

'I remember it – Sir Walter Loddington.'

'Sir Walter!' Will Kemp exclaimed. 'We know of him. He is a man of great wealth indeed – but poor reputation. They say that the queen has refused to raise him up to be a baron and he has borne a grudge ever since.'

'Aye,' said Master Shakespeare. 'Rumour has it that his friends in Spain would pay him a fortune to rid them of the queen and put a Spanish king on the throne.'

Alice struggled to her feet. 'His servant was in on it too,' she insisted. 'He had a scar on his face and a crooked eye that looked the wrong way. He was a cruel, evil man. He was the one that beat me.'

Will Kemp took Alice's hand. 'Tell me, do you have proof of this plot to poison the queen?'

Alice shook her head. 'Only what I heard.'

Master Shakespeare shrugged and began to pace the floor, tapping his chin as he pondered on the problem. 'Without proof it is difficult to do anything. But we go to the palace tomorrow and I shall speak of it.'

'You can do no more,' said Will Kemp.

Then Master Shakespeare looked at Alice. 'Now I understand how you have suffered, and I shall forgive your lies, Barnaby…er, Alice.'

Overjoyed, she leaped up and flung her arms around Master Shakespeare's neck squealing, 'Thank you! Thank you!' before she pulled herself together, pink with embarrassment, and said, 'I promise I'll perform my very best for the queen, sir.'

'Perform? No! No! No!' Master Shakespeare roared, shaking his head violently. 'Do you want to see me in the Tower? If you're found to be a maid, I will be finished. I say again, it is against the law.'

Master Kemp rested his hand on Master Shakespeare's shoulder. 'William,' he said quietly, 'we have no time to find a lad to play Beatrice. We perform for Her Majesty tomorrow.'

Master Shakespeare looked as if he had lost a shilling and found a farthing. 'Then what shall we do?' he asked.

'Just think,' Master Kemp replied. 'All these weeks, no one guessed that Barnaby was a girl, did they?'

'No, they didn't.'

'Not even you.'

'No, but…'

'Well then,' the comic continued. 'Consider this: tomorrow, this maid will perform her part. No one but you, Thomas and I will know she is not Barnaby. She can leave the following day.'

'And what of my family, sir?' asked Alice. 'Can they stay here?'

But Master Shakespeare's temper flared up again and his face flushed scarlet. 'Nay, have I not done enough? You are expecting too much of me. Send your mother away. She can look after her boys,' he said and turned his back on her.

Alice was furious and ran round to face him, 'Send 'em away?' she shouted. 'I won't do no such thing! They're in as much danger from that apothecary as I am. They can stay here or—'

Now it was Master Shakespeare's turn to shout. 'Or what, my girl? What will you do? Will you go to the magistrate?'

Alice was silent for a second and then she said, 'No. But I will go with my mother and brothers. I will walk out of here and then who will play your Beatrice for the queen?'

The playwright stood there, colour draining from his cheeks, not knowing what to say.

Master Kemp stepped forward. 'Let them stay, Will. They are all in danger if they return to the city. What harm can they do here? Let them stay until the play is done. The maid is right. There is no time to find another for the part of Beatrice.'

In the end Master Shakespeare agreed that they could stay and that Willum and Jack could take small non-speaking parts in *Much Ado About Nothing*. 'And you, mistress, must not be left alone,' he said, waving at Alice's mother. 'You will come with us to the Palace.'

Mother Trowte bent her creaking knees and made a strange, wobbly curtsey. 'I thank you, sir,' she said, her eyes twinkling. 'But what part shall I play?'

He stared at her and then a smile broke across his face. 'There are no fairies in this play, madam,' he joked, 'and so I'm afraid there is not a part for you.'

We all tittered and so did Mother Trowte.

Will Kemp walked towards her. 'If anyone asks you why you are with the Chamberlain's Men,' he grinned, 'tell them you are Master Shakespeare's laundry maid.' And we laughed and clapped such a fine suggestion.

When the rehearsal began again, Willum and Jack played their parts well. They stood where they were told to stand and didn't make any trouble. Mother Trowte slouched in a chair, scratching her legs or picking her nose and occasionally nodding off. But most of the time she watched our perform- ance – laughing at Master Kemp's antics as Dogberry and clapping and shouting like any good audience.

When we were finished, I took the Trowte family to the lodging house, where we all lay together, packed tight as apples in a barrel. Even so, the straw mattresses were a good deal more comfortable than the baker's floor had been the night before and we all slept soundly.

Tomorrow was an important day. We must be ready to perform for the queen.

Chapter 28

The Man with the Scar

The day of the performance arrived grey and bitterly cold. Snow was falling while the cart with its high sides stood outside the Curtain waiting to be loaded.

'Wrap up warm!' called Master Burbage, who always worried about his voice. 'We want no one taking a chill before we reach the Palace.' He picked up his thick woollen cloak and wrapped it around his shoulders and half his face before stepping outside.

Once we had heaved trunks of costumes onto the cart and topped them with an assortment of props and several folded scene cloths, Roger fetched the horses and backed them between the shafts. When that was done, we were ready to go, apart from the problem of Mother Trowte, who couldn't walk with the rest of us on account of her troublesome feet.

'If you give me a heave-ho, I'll sit myself up there,' she said, pointing to a space at the back of the cart. Then she beckoned Roger and me to come and help. 'You're a pair of strong lads,' she said as she flung her arms around our shoulders. Give me a good push now.'

So we shoved as hard as we could and she scrambled onto the cart with a good deal of *oopsing* and *oohing* and *ahhhing*. Once she'd flopped down and made herself comfortable among the bags of periwigs, Master Shakespeare raised his arm and beckoned us to go.

We set off, walking alongside the cart. Willum and Jack were very excited by the whole adventure and walked with Master Kemp who was happy to keep them amused with his jigs and funny stories and silly songs.

Before long the snow was falling so thickly that we could scarcely see ahead through the white mist. As we passed by Bishopsgate and on into the city people were hurrying through the streets to escape the cold, and those who stayed and attempted to sell their wares were huddled in doorways sheltering from the snow and the keen wind.

With the horses slipping and sliding on the cobbles, we passed through the city and left by Ludgate and on over the Fleet River. Luckily it was frozen and we didn't have to suffer the terrible stink of rotting flesh that I remembered from when I first arrived in London. Even so, I couldn't help pinching my nose – just in case.

The snow storm continued as the cart rumbled across the bridge and along Fleet Street. By this time the Chamberlain's Men were a comical sight – white from head to foot, like a troupe of ghosts on the march. And Mother Trowte, sitting on the cart with her shawl pulled over her head, was so thickly covered in snow that she looked like a marble statue.

Alice and I plodded on with our heads cast down to keep the icy flakes out of our eyes. 'Look now!' Roger called to us over his shoulder. 'Whitehall Palace! You can see it.'

We raised our hands and shielded our eyes and, to our surprise, we saw that there was not just one palace but a great many buildings spread out in front of us.

Alice squealed, 'Oh, *aaah*! Don't it look grand, Thomas? But it's more like a town. So many buildings, ain't there? Does the queen live in all of 'em?'

'How would I know?' I said as we walked on beside the cart.

'Perhaps she's got a big family. Uncles and cousins and that. Otherwise it don't make sense to have all them rooms. She can only sleep in one bed at a time, that's what I say.'

'I suppose a queen needs palaces,' I said. 'She has to impress people and show how wealthy she is and how important.'

Alice went quiet and tugged at my sleeve. 'I ain't never seen the queen,' she whispered. 'Now we're getting near, my knees are a-knocking like turnips in a pot.'

I laughed. 'I don't suppose the queen will speak to us. I think she'll only talk to rich people.'

This seemed to make her feel better, until we arrived at the palace gates where we were faced with guards, dressed in scarlet uniforms, crossing their pikes to prevent us from entering.

'Halt! Who goes there?' one called as if we were a band of brigands.

Alice gasped at the sight of them. 'They look ever so fierce. Will they send us to the stocks?'

But Master Shakespeare marched confidently to the front of our troupe. 'We are the Lord Chamberlain's Men,' he called in a bold voice. 'We are here to entertain Her Majesty.' The guards raised their pikes immediately which made us feel very important.

As we walked across a flat area beyond the gates, Roger turned to us and grinned. 'How do you like this?' he said. 'This is the tiltyard. This is where knights charge on their horses, knocking each other to the ground with lances.'

I snorted. 'That's a dangerous way to pass the time.'

'No!' Roger insisted. 'They say it's a great entertainment. Her Majesty likes to watch.'

Alice thumped his shoulder. 'If men are foolish enough to want to kill each other, I'm ashamed that a queen likes to watch it.'

Roger, who didn't agree, turned away in a sulk.

A gentleman dressed in black velvet appeared from nowhere and walked straight up to Master Shakespeare.

'Welcome, Master Shakespeare,' he said.

'Master Tilney,' our leader replied, nervously nodding his head in a sort of bow. 'I am honoured to be asked to perform for Her Majesty once more.'

Master Tilney nodded. 'I hope Her Majesty will enjoy your performance more than the Admiral's Men's play yesterday. It was about Robin Hood.' He frowned and shook his head. 'Not good. Not good.'

I nudged Roger. 'Who's that?' I asked. 'Is he important?'

'He's Edmund Tilney. Master of Revels,' he whispered forgetting his sulk, pleased to show off his knowledge of the queen's court. 'Master Tilney checks all the new plays in the land. You've got to watch out for him. He can stop a play being performed, if he's a mind to.

'You can tell that Master Shakespeare ain't pleased the Admiral's Men have been invited this year. He likes to be the main attraction.'

We didn't care about the Admiral's Men or anything else for that matter. We were standing in the freezing cold and we all wanted to get inside.

Unfortunately the man in black didn't seem to notice us poor shivering wretches. 'I read your new play, Master Shakespeare, and found it excellent. No problems with this one, I think.' Then he wagged his finger. 'Though there were things in *Richard II* which affronted Her Majesty, I'm afraid.'

Master Shakespeare blushed. 'For which I apologise, sir. I did not mean to displease her. But I think this play will amuse.'

'Indeed, indeed,' said the Master of Revels, holding out his hand and pointing to a great oak door. 'Follow me, if you will.' And with that, he spun round and walked at a brisk pace into the palace. Meanwhile, we each lifted bundles and boxes off the cart and carried them on our shoulders. Some of the guards picked up the things that were left and followed on behind.

Master Tilney led us down long, wood-panelled corridors where the walls were hung with fine portraits.

'Kings and queens and knights,' whispered Roger and, as we passed through, he pointed out weird and wonderful presents given to the queen from all over the world. There was a Madonna made of Indian feathers, and a unicorn's tail, and chairs painted with gold. There was even a mirror so enormous that I could see myself in it from top to toe. But who wants to look at himself? That's what I say.

'It don't seem right, do it, Thomas?' Alice commented as we turned down yet another corridor. 'All these things just for a queen when poor folk go hungry.'

'No,' said Mother Trowte who was trying to keep up as best she could. 'I could get a good price for one of them chairs. Feed us for a year, it would.'

Roger looked round, his face filled with horror. '*Shhh!*' he hissed. 'None of your talk, Mistress Trowte! 'Tis treason. If anyone hears, you'll have us all sent down to the dungeons.'

By then, the Master of Revels had turned the last corner and led us through two enormous doors into the great chamber, which was already ablaze with torches and candles especially for the occasion.

'*Ooooh!* So this is where we'll perform!' cried Alice as we set down the boxes of props and scenery cloths. 'You could fit half of Cripplegate in here! And look at them!' she squealed pointing up at the huge hangings on the wall. I'd never seen such things before, either.

'They're tapestries,' Master Kemp explained before Roger could jump in. 'They are very fine indeed – made by Flemish weavers. Old King Henry, the queen's father, had them brought here in ships.'

I didn't know where Flemish weavers lived but I thought it must be far away. They were certainly very clever to make such pictures on their looms. Horses, deer, maidens and scenes of forests. Amazing!

We stood and gaped at them until Alice spotted something else at the far end of the room. 'What's that?' she asked, pointing to an enormous chair set on a plinth – carved and decorated and painted gold with a grand canopy above. 'Is that the queen's throne, Master Kemp?'

He nodded. 'Her Majesty will sit there while her guests sit on the benches at the side of the room,' he told us. 'It will be a splendid sight. But come now, we must get ready.'

My heart beat faster at those words. It was nearly time to perform before the queen. I could only hope that I would remember my lines and act well.

Master Tilney showed us to a small, square room, which we would use as a tiring room to change our clothes. Alice put on a blue silk dress and a periwig of long fair hair while I squeezed into a hideous pink frock covered in forget-me-nots. I hoped that it would not be long before I grew too tall to play the part of a girl.

In less than an hour all was ready. The scenery was set up and we were dressed in our costumes, ready to begin.

Jack and Willum were bubbling with excitement so, as soon as we were allowed, we took them to the doorway which led onto the space that we would use for a stage. The entrance was hung with heavy curtains of red and gold and we peeped through the gap in the middle to see the great chamber. It was a sight so grand that Jack and Willum squealed with delight as we watched the guests arrive, all in their finest clothes to impress the queen, and take their seats.

'*Ooooh, ah!* See them rich folk in their silks,' cried Jack. 'I ain't never seen such jewels, and look at them wide skirts. You'd think they couldn't get through the doors!'

'*Oooh*, look at them shoes! They're bootiful!' squealed Willum, who had never worn shoes in his life until Master Shakespeare gave him a pair from the costume box.

Apart from the clothes, we marvelled at the periwigs which were huge and colourful and often studded with pearls.

'Why ain't Ma got one?' asked Willum, who didn't know the cost of things. 'Ma would look bootiful in a periwig.'

Jack leaned forward to answer in a way Willum would understand. 'It's a well-known fact,' he said, 'that fleas and rats live in them periwigs, see.'

Willum looked at Jack, his eyes wide and serious. 'Ma don't like fleas and rats, does she, Jack?'

'That's right, she don't. They makes her itch.'

Satisfied with this explanation, Willum grinned. 'Then we don't want wigs in our house, do we?'

To our surprise, we saw Master Shakespeare walk into the great chamber and mingle with the guests, bowing to the ladies, smiling and shaking hands with the gentlemen and spending time in conversation.

Gradually the audience settled themselves on the benches, talking with other guests, while their servants stood behind, leaning against the walls. And Master Shakespeare left the room as six yeomen of the guard entered. They were a fine sight, dressed in red with gilt buttons and embroidery as they came marching into the great chamber to take their places on either side of the throne.

As if that was not enough, the most exciting thing of all happened next. At the far end of the room, trumpets sounded loud and long. The guests grew silent. There was not a murmur, not a shuffle to be heard, for everyone knew that the queen was about to enter.

'I'm all of a quiver,' whispered Alice from behind the curtain. 'I daren't look!' And she clapped her hands over her eyes.

'I daren't, neither,' said Jack and did the same.

'Me an' all!' Willum squealed and copied Jack.

But as the queen stepped into the room, I saw them spread their fingers little by little and peep between them.

'She ain't as big as I thought,' hissed Jack.

'She's very little,' said Willum. 'No bigger than Alice.'

The guests bowed and curtseyed low as she moved slowly down the room, her head held high, her scarlet gown rustling as she walked. A long string of pearls hung down the front of her dress while her neck was encased in the most enormous ruff embroidered with silver thread and edged with even more pearls.

'Lovely little hands she's got,' Alice marvelled. 'Not rough like mine. And see that ring she's wearing. All diamonds and rubies. Ain't it fine?'

But the boys saw things differently.

'I can't believe it!' said Jack. 'She's the queen and she's really old – older than Ma even. The queen shouldn't be old.'

Willum nodded in agreement.

'And, see! She's limping.'

'Has she got bunions, Jack?' asked Willum.

'Probably,' Jack replied. 'And I bet she's bald under that periwig, for all the jewels she sticks in it. Mark my words, she ain't got no hair.'

Willum frowned. 'She ain't suffering from the plague, is she, Jack? Her face is as white as paper.'

'Don't talk such silliness,' hissed Alice, 'That's special stuff she puts on her face, if you must know. It's white lead and vinegar to make her skin look beautiful. I expect only queens can afford it.'

This explanation puzzled Jack. 'Then why's she got splodges of red paint on her cheeks?'

'And her mouth,' said Willum.

Alice sighed, irritated by her brothers' ignorance. 'Oh, you boys don't understand,' she snapped. ''Tis the fashion.'

Once the queen had reached the throne, she arranged her skirt and settled on the cushioned seat before raising her hand and giving the signal for the performance to begin.

By this time, of course, all the actors had joined us behind the curtains ready to walk into the great chamber and start the play. But first a drum roll sounded and continued until any chatter had died down and you could hear a pin drop. Then Master Shakespeare stepped briskly onto the stage and bowed low.

'I am honoured to present my humble play *Much Ado About Nothing* to Your Majesty,' he said, speaking in a bold voice which must have impressed the queen and her guests. He explained a little bit about the play (which was very complicated and all about love, as usual), and when he had finished he bowed again and stepped aside.

Then the musicians began to play gentle music which was the cue for Alice and me – Beatrice and Hero – to walk on, dressed in long silk dresses, with Master Burbage and Roger by our sides.

We were shaking with nerves. Acting in front of the queen was a terrifying thing. But I took a deep breath and spoke my first words.

Chapter 29
A Terrible Wedding

It was clear that the audience were enjoying the play – they were laughing a good deal. Then, in the middle of the third act, I saw Alice's face suddenly turn white as paper and she glanced across at me, her eyes filled with fear. I was alarmed. *What could have happened to make her so scared?* I wondered.

Once the third act had ended and we were leaving the great chamber Alice grabbed my arm and pulled me aside.

'Thomas, I've seen them!'

'Who?'

'That evil man, Sir Walter Loddington. Him what bought the poison. Him what cut my hair. Oh, my stars! He is seated by that big tapestry, Thomas, all dressed up in a fine blue robe with a great ruby ring an' all. Did you see him?'

Now I understood why she looked so frightened. But I hadn't seen this man – for how could I recognise someone I had never met?

Alice was all of a dither. 'His servant – him what beat me to an inch of my life – he was standing behind Sir Walter. I feel sick at the sight of him, I do,' she said and she leaned on the wall and closed her eyes.

'Calm yourself, Alice. We'll go to Master Shakespeare and you can tell him what you saw. He'll know what to do.'

Together we hurried to the tiring room, which was packed

with sweating bodies, pulling off shirts and jerkins of one colour to exchange them for another and swapping caps and periwigs to look completely different for the next act. Master Shakespeare was on the far side bending over and tugging at Master Burbage's boots which were much too small. We pushed our way across the crowded room to reach him.

As we approached he looked up and frowned. 'Why have you not changed?' he barked. 'Go and get ready for the next act. We cannot keep Her Majesty waiting.'

'Sir,' I said, leaning forward and speaking into his ear. 'Barnaby has seen the two men.'

He stared at me. 'What are you talking about, Thomas? Which men?'

'Sir Walter Loddington and his—' Alice said.

Suddenly realising who she had seen, Master Shakespeare spun round and held his hand across her mouth. 'Say no more, Barnaby,' he whispered and grasped us both by the arm before tugging us towards a corner where we could talk without being overheard.

'Now tell me what you saw, Barnaby.'

'That so-called gentleman Sir Walter Loddington, him what bought the poison. And his roguish servant is with him.'

'Are you sure?'

'I'm sure as eggs is eggs, sir. They are in the great chamber, by the big tapestry,' she said and began to tremble. 'Oh, my lawd! What if he poisons the queen? What shall we do?'

'I spoke to a guard as we came into the palace but I'm afraid he laughed.' Master Shakespeare shook his head. 'There are a dozen tales of plots every day, he said. He asked if I had proof but I couldn't give him any.'

Then he raised his hand and beckoned Will Kemp to come over and repeated what Alice had told him.

'So Sir Walter is in the audience,' said Will Kemp. 'Then we must stop him.'

'Let us think about this,' said Master Shakespeare rubbing his chin, pondering. 'Her Majesty is safe and well guarded in the great chamber. If we make a fuss, the celebrations will be ruined and the queen will not be pleased. Sir Walter and his man are no danger to anyone while they sit there. I think we must wait until the play is finished.'

'What then?'

'While you are performing your dance, Will, I will go and find Master Tilney. He has the ear of the queen and he will take notice of me. I shall tell him what Barnaby has seen. I don't doubt he will have plenty of questions to ask Sir Walter and his man. The act of buying poison is against the law. If his plot should involve the queen, well...'

Master Shakespeare's plan was a good one. Nobody would leave the chamber before Master Kemp had finished his dance, for the audiences loved to watch him. He was well-known for his dances and he performed one after every play. So it was agreed that while he was dancing and jigging about, Master Shakespeare would look for Master Tilney.

'If he finds that Sir Walter has plotted to poison the queen, he will be taken to the dungeons,' said Master Shakespeare, rubbing his hands gleefully at the thought of a cold, rat-infested prison. 'It is no more than that treacherous man deserves.'

In spite of all our worries, we began the last act of *Much Ado About Nothing*. As we stepped into the great chamber I scanned the audience for Sir Walter and saw him – a bald, big-bellied men in a blue robe – and behind him was his servant with a long scar across his cheek, just as Alice had described. He looked like a man to be afraid of.

The play was going well. The audience were enjoying themselves and, from time to time, I saw Her Majesty rocking with laughter. That would please Master Shakespeare indeed.

All went smoothly, until right at the end – the wedding scene.

Alice was wearing a long dress of white silk which draped on the floor at the back. It was Jack and Willum's job to hold the dress off the ground so that she wouldn't trip. They walked behind her in their blue satin doublets and white satin caps, drawing *oohs* and *ahhhs* from the audience. Being so young, they appealed to the ladies in particular. The boys seemed very pleased with themselves and they did their best to stand in the right place and move when they were supposed to move and not bump into the actors.

The problem was Willum. Being only seven years old, he soon grew bored and, while the real actors were saying their parts, he shuffled about a good deal, as small boys will, and accidentally stepped on the hem of Alice's dress.

This wouldn't have mattered except that when Alice stepped forward, that's when the accident happened. Because her dress was trapped under Willum's feet, she was pulled off balance and tumbled backwards, sprawling across the floor in one direction while her periwig went in the other, revealing her cropped red hair.

The audience fell about laughing, thinking it was a fine joke, and when Alice scrambled across the floor, snatched up the periwig and put it back on, they laughed even more and clapped as she stood up and carried on with the scene.

But it was no joke. It was the worst thing that could have happened.

While all this was going on, I had kept my eyes fixed on Sir Walter and, when Alice's periwig was knocked off, I saw his jaw drop and his face grow pale as he clearly recognised her.

For some time his eyes followed her movements across the stage. Then he lifted his hand and beckoned to his servant who bent over to listen to what his master had to say. All the time Sir Walter was speaking they were both watching Alice. Then Sir Walter turned and placed something in his servant's hand. The servant bowed briefly and, to my horror, edged towards the door until, seconds later, he had disappeared from the great chamber.

Chapter 30
Arrested

When the play finally ended, we bowed to the audience until the applause faded, then walked out of the great chamber, leaving it to Master Kemp and his dance.

Alice knew nothing of what I had seen and, as soon as we were in the corridor, I pulled her to one side. 'You are in danger,' I said. 'Sir Walter recognised you when your periwig fell off. He sent his servant from the room and I believe he'll come looking for you.'

Poor Alice. Her face turned deathly pale and she grasped my hand. 'Oh gawd! Oh Heavens! We must tell Master Shakespeare at once.'

We hurried to the tiring room where the actors were taking off their costumes ready to leave the Palace. Roger was there, half naked, struggling to get out of a pair of silk breeches.

'Where is Master Shakespeare?' I called to him but he merely shrugged, 'Dunno.'

'We need to speak with him, Roger,' I insisted. 'It's urgent.'

'Ask Master Burbage. He'll know where he is,' he replied as he folded his costume into a large trunk.

Mother Trowte, who was sitting nearby called, 'Master Burbage is over there,' and flapped her hand towards the far corner before turning away to catch hold of Willum who was standing on a chair, poking Jack with a wooden sword.

We pushed our way across the crowded room where we found Master Burbage. He was still dressed in his costume, seated on a bench and bent over with his head in his hands.

'Sir!' I said, standing in front of him. 'Do you know where Master Shakespeare is? I must speak with him urgently.'

He raised his head slowly, and I was shocked to see that his brow was furrowed and his face was grey with worry. 'He is with the queen's guards, Thomas.' He spoke softly as if he were speaking to himself. 'I fear something is amiss. But it surely cannot be that the queen did not like our play. We acted well, I'll swear. I saw her laugh more than once.'

Alice sat down beside him. 'No, Master Burbage. They all liked the play – and your acting. That ain't the reason,' she said. 'You tell 'im, Thomas. Tell 'im what Master Shakespeare's doing.'

Master Burbage looked up at me. 'What do you know, Thomas? Tell me!'

'Master Shakespeare has important information for the queen,' I said. 'After the play was done, he went to find Master Tilney so that Her Majesty would know of a terrible danger that could threaten her life.'

At first the man's eyes grew wide with the shock of what I had told him but then his forehead creased into a puzzled expression. 'I don't understand,' he said. 'If that is so, why did the queen's guards drag him away down the corridor? Why have they commanded us to remain in the tiring room?' He shook his head. 'No, Thomas, I fear he has been arrested –

though I do not know why. But I must tell our troupe what has happened.'

Master Burbage got to his feet and pushed his way into the middle of the room and stood on a chair, clapping his hands for quiet until the whole troupe – some in their under-garments – stood still, looking across at him, wondering what was so important.

'Move, Alice,' I hissed. 'We're wasting time, come on.' I gave her a push and we hurried towards the door, leaving Master Burbage addressing the actors.

'But I don't understand, Thomas. Why have they had Master Shakespeare arrested? Why him?'

'Because Sir Walter Loddington is a clever man. He doubt-less has a trick up his sleeve. The sooner we talk to Master Tilney the better. Before the guards take Master Shakespeare away.'

'To the Tower?'

'Heaven help him.'

Still dressed as Beatrice and Hero, we raced along the deserted corridor, hoping to find somebody to talk to. Down the panelled hallway we went, past the paintings of kings and queens, and past the Madonna made of feathers.

When we turned the next corner, we almost bumped into two yeomen guarding a door. They were holding their halberds upright until they saw us and then they shouted, 'Ho! Who goes there?' and swung their weapons low, baring the way ahead.

I stood in front of them, pulling myself up to my full height. 'We have been sent to find Master Tilney,' I said in my best grown-up voice. 'We need to speak to him about Master Shakespeare. It is most important. Please take us to him at once.'

The guards raised their halberds but they did not let us pass as I had hoped. The taller of the two looked down from his great height, his chin pulled into his neck like an old cockerel.

'*Aaah!*' he said, raising his eyebrows. 'You was one of them ruffians acting in the play, wasn't you?' He looked across at the other guard and winked. 'So you want to know about Master Shakespeare, do yer?' He bent forward until we were nose to nose then he spoke in a low growly voice. 'Well, he's down below in his own private quarters with some fine locks on the door. And you ain't allowed down there – unless you wants to be locked up with him.' His mouth twisted into a smirk. 'But I don't think you'd like the rats, would yer? They're giant rats, they are!'

I wasn't bothered by his jibes. 'We have something to say,' I insisted. 'We need to speak to someone important.'

This was a mistake. The guard straightened up, his face turning scarlet. 'I am important!' he bellowed. 'Now get back with the rest of them rogues where you belongs.'

He swung the long shaft of his halberd so that the spike pointed at us as if he was about to run us through, and we had no choice but to scurry back down the corridor to the tiring room where two guards were now standing at the door.

'What you two vagabonds doing out here?' one asked.

'None of your business,' snapped Alice, and we pushed

191

passed them into the room where the Chamberlain's Men were waiting.

Roger came hurrying over. 'Where've you been?' he hissed. 'I've got somethink to tell you, I have,' and he bent forward, pulling us into a small circle.

'Master Shakespeare's been taken to the cells.'

'We know,' I said.

'Did you know he's been accused of stealing? He'll hang, he will!'

We stood with mouths agape, shocked at the news.

'He ain't no thief,' Alice protested. 'Who said he was?'

'They say some poxy servant said he'd seen him pinch a ruby ring from Sir Walter Loddington.'

'I don't believe a word of it,' said Alice.

'Nor me,' Roger replied. 'But Sir Walter is as mad as the devil. He's going to question us all. He believes Master Shakespeare passed the ring to one of us.'

Alice looked grim as she turned to me. 'This is how he will get to me, Thomas. He knows what I saw and heard. Somehow he will find a way to have me killed.'

Chapter 31

'I Ain't Never Seen a Queen!'

The Chamberlain's Men were a sorry sight, sitting silently on benches or cross-legged on the floor, their faces glum, their chins cupped in their hands. They had been told of Master Shakespeare's arrest and were commanded not to leave the palace but to remain in the tiring room.

Mother Trowte was the only one standing, and when she saw us she limped over at top speed, her shawl flapping like bats' wings.

'Where you been?' she demanded, shaking Alice's arm vigorously. 'What you lot up to, eh? Leaving me here like that, not knowing where you was.'

We explained what we had tried to do.

'Well, it didn't work, did it?' she said waspishly. 'You stay here with me and you don't do nothing.'

'But, Ma,' protested Alice. 'The queen must learn about Gideon de Laine and the poison. She must!'

The old lady slumped onto a box and sat there, picking at a wart on her nose while she thought of a solution. 'Well,' she said at last. 'A cat may look at a queen, so they say.'

Alice had no idea what her mother meant and she turned her eyes to the ceiling in exasperation.

Jack was just as puzzled. 'What you mean, Ma?' he asked.

Mother Trowte looked at him and winked. 'Who is it that needs to know about that there poison?'

Silence.

'Who's right next door, eh?' she said wrapping her arms across her chest, her lips set in a smug smile as she waited for us to reply. And when we didn't she said, 'Her Majesty the queen, that's who!'

We looked at each other and shrugged. Of course the queen needed to know the truth. Of course she was in the next room. Her Majesty and her guests had already started dancing. We could hear the music.

'I got a plan, see,' Ma whispered.

Alice sank to the floor, her head in her hands. 'Not another plan! Your plans are dangerous.'

'Let's listen, Alice,' I said. 'We can give it a try. What have we got to lose?'

Alice leaped to her feet. 'What have we got to lose?' she shrieked. 'Our heads, that's what! Fancy yours on a spike, do yer?'

But when Mother Trowte told us her idea, I thought it was a good one. Alice did not but, once she had stopped pulling faces and protesting and pacing around the room, she agreed to try it.

So we set the plan into action.

The tiring room was full of unhappy actors, waiting for news of what was to happen to Master Shakespeare. The costumes had been packed, the props had been put in boxes, and the scene cloths folded. There was nothing for them to do but sit and hope that all would be well. But suddenly Mother Trowte began to moan and then she stood up, gasping for breath.

'It's too hot in here,' she wheezed, flapping her hand across her face. 'Oh my! I need fresh air, I do. I'm sweating fit to drop.' And she staggered across to the door and opened it. 'Fresh air, for pity's sake!' she wailed.

Two of the queen's guards were standing at the door, dressed in red uniforms as alike as two holly berries. 'You can't leave the room, mistress,' one said. 'We are here on the queen's command.'

As they tried to close the door Mother Trowte flung her arms in the air and sobbed, 'Then I shall die for want of breath.' She let out a terrifying moan and collapsed forward so that the door couldn't be shut without chopping her in half.

'She's my ma, she is!' Jack yelled at the guards.

'Pick her up, can't yer?' screamed Alice. 'The queen won't like it if she dies in her palace.'

By then most of the actors had come to see what was going on.

The one guard looked at the other. 'We'd better help the old baggage, George. Come on, give us a hand.' And the two of them bent down and tried to lift Mother Trowte by the arms but she gave them no help and dangled lifelessly between them like a string puppet.

'She's dying, she is!' shouted Alice, tugging the guards by their sleeves. 'Take her to that window, quick. If she gets a bit of cold air she could be right as rain.'

Alice, Jack and most of the actors insisted on going down the corridor with them, which slowed the guards no end. Meanwhile Willum and I slipped, unnoticed, out of the tiring room and headed the other way.

We ran along the corridor until we came to a corner.

'Hide under that chair, Willum,' I said, pointing to a large oak carver set against the wall. 'Don't say a word.'

Willum nodded and squeezed himself beneath the chair while I kneeled on the floor and poked my head round the corner to see if the coast was clear. It wasn't. More guards were posted on the entrance to the great chamber. I stood up and took a deep breath before turning the corner and running towards the guards. 'Help!' I called with great urgency. 'George asked me to come. He needs help.'

'Did he?' said one guard. 'What's up?'

'Woman near to dying,' I panted. 'They're trying to bring her back to life. Said I was to tell you to come and help. Didn't want Her Majesty to hear of it.'

The guards, who had been standing at the door for hours, were glad of a bit of drama and set off running, leaving their halberds leaning against the wall.

As soon as they had gone, Willum scrambled out from under the chair. I took a folded a bit of paper from my pocket and handed it to him. 'Give this to Her Majesty and remember what you have to say.'

Willum grinned, not looking at all nervous, and I wondered if he really understood how important this was. For a few seconds we listened to the trumpets and sackbuts playing for the queen's guests as they danced, then I flung open the door and gave Willum a hefty push which sent him headlong into the room. His legs stumbled, his little arms flailed in the air until he finally went crashing into a stout lady dancing with an even stouter gentleman.

The lady collapsed screaming, not knowing what strange object had collided with her. Then other ladies there abouts started a-screeching and a-wailing. Gentlemen began to shout and pushed forward to see what was going on. The musicians stopped playing and stared.

All was chaos until some of the yeomen guarding the queen came rushing forward with their halberds at the ready and the crowd parted to make way.

What a shock when the closest saw that the cause of all the commotion was pint-sized Willum standing alone and staring wide-eyed as the guards surrounded him.

'We have an intruder,' boomed one of them and, at this announcement, four more guards arrived dashing in through another door.

'Take him away,' the guard commanded, pointing at Willum who suddenly looked terrified and burst into tears.

'I only wanted to see the queen,' he wailed, rubbing his eyes. 'I ain't never seen a queen.'

The noise in the room suddenly turned to titters as everyone realised that the panic was caused by a very small boy. Then the titters turned to laughter and he stood there confused until someone said, 'So, the young gentleman wants to see the queen, does he?'

Just like everyone else, I gasped when I saw Her Majesty walking towards Willum who suddenly stopped crying and stared with his mouth wide open.

'Take care, Your Majesty,' said one of the guards, his halberd pointing at Willum.

But the queen laughed and pushed it aside. 'And what harm can a small boy do? Are we afraid of children now?'

The guard looked embarrassed and stepped away while she walked forward until she was no more than a pace from Willum.

'And what do you think of your queen?' she said gazing down at him. 'How do you like her?' Then she smiled, and I was shocked to see that her teeth were black and rotten. It was obvious she had never taken advantage of Master Grimbald's skills with false teeth.

I waited behind the door, peeping through the gap to see if Willum would do as we had asked him to. Would he remember? Would he be too scared? Would the guards take him?

'What is your name?' the queen asked bending forward.

'W-Willum,' he stuttered, wiping away the tears with his hand. 'I've got something for you, Y-Your Majesty.'

He pulled out the note I had written, and the queen held out her hand to take it. That was when I saw her ring – just as Alice had said – with a letter E set in diamonds that flashed in the light of all the candles. Amazing!

The queen slowly unfolded the paper. Maybe she thought he had brought her a poem. I expect people often did.

'Have you written this for me, young sir?' she asked. 'I thank you.'

Willum, not knowing how to reply, said nothing.

For a minute the queen squinted as if she couldn't see the words clearly, and then she smiled and read the first line out loud.

'Your Majesty, I am your humble and devoted servant.' But as she read the next, her face suddenly blackened. 'I wish to warn you that you are in terrible danger.' Shaking with rage, she flung the paper away as if it were a red-hot coal. 'A trick!' she roared. 'How dare you enter my presence with this? Master Secretary, come and deal with this child.'

A man suddenly appeared from nowhere. He was small with short legs and a crooked back. He had the most terrifying dark eyes and a black beard as pointed as any dagger.

The queen, who was now in a dreadful temper, snapped at him. 'Find who is behind this letter,' she demanded. 'By Heaven I will not be made a fool of by one so young.' She glared at Willum and pointed to the man with the crooked back. 'This is Robert Cecil, child, Secretary of State and the most important man in the land. Don't play the fool with him or you will suffer for it!' Then she looked at Robert Cecil and said, 'When you have sorted out this trouble, come and report to my privy chamber at once.' With that she turned away and marched from the room, snorting like an angry bull.

The Secretary of State began his questioning at once. 'Your name, boy,' he demanded.

By then Willum was too scared to speak and was shaking so badly that I couldn't bear to watch. I burst into the room and ran to help him. At the same time, Alice came rushing through the other door too fast for the guards to stop her and flung herself in front of Robert Cecil.

'He don't mean no harm, sir,' she said. 'It's just that Master Shakespeare has been arrested, see.'

'I am aware of that. I have had him placed in a cell and I am like to send you to join him.'

'But he ain't no thief, sir,' she whispered. 'It's all the fault of them poisoners that was watching the play. They're right here in this room, they are. We thought Her Majesty should know about 'em, and—'

But Robert Cecil held up his hand for silence.

'Quiet, you impudent youth,' he said before looking around him and calling. 'Who is in charge of these young actors?'

Mother Trowte had recovered miraculously from her fainting fit and had followed Alice into the chamber. She stepped forward, did a wobbly curtsy and said, 'Willum's mine, sir.'

At the sight of Mother Trowte, Robert Cecil held a kerchief to his nose, clearly uncomfortable at being near to a poor old crone. Then he herded us all to a far corner near the stage so as not to be overheard by the guests.

'Explain what these youths are up to if you can, woman.'

She curtseyed again. 'Well, it's like this, sir,' she said, speaking in a low voice, 'There was this apothi-what's-it what sold poison to a gent and his servant what beat up our—'

Alice interrupted. 'The gentleman is planning to put the poison on a pair of earrings and give them as a gift to the queen.'

'It would get in her ear 'ole, see,' said Mother Trowte, sticking a finger into her own ear as a demonstration, 'and then she'd be...a goner!'

All this time there was a great deal of murmuring from the ladies and gentlemen in the room who were wondering what was going on. Robert Cecil turned to me and leaned forward. 'Do you know the name of the gentleman who bought the poison?'

'We do, sir,' I whispered, 'for he is in this very room. He is Sir Walter Loddington. They say he is in league with the Spanish in a plot to kill the queen.'

Robert Cecil looked grim. 'Indeed, there are rumours of such plots – though I have no proof.' He paused for a moment, pressing his fingers to his mouth before saying, 'If there is a traitor among us, we shall find him.' He turned to the guards standing near. 'Follow me! We must find Sir Walter Loddington, for I have serious questions to ask.'

There was a buzzing in the great chamber, which grew louder as the Secretary of State marched across the room, followed by four guards. The crowd parted to make way for them as they headed towards the far end where Sir Walter was standing stock still, his eyes wide and fixed on Sir Robert Cecil as he approached, like a rabbit caught in a trap. But, before the guards reached him, he seemed to wake from his trance and he suddenly turned and bolted for the door.

'Seize him!' Robert Cecil roared, and the guards, who were younger and faster than Sir Walter, were on him before he was halfway across the room. They grabbed hold of his arms and dragged him roughly towards the Secretary of State where he fell to his knees, cowering.

Chapter 32
Snowball

Every eye in the room was fixed on Sir Walter as he kneeled before Robert Cecil, his head bent low, shaking like a frightened dog. 'I assure you, sir, I know nothing of any poison.'

Robert Cecil frowned. 'I have reason to believe that you did,' he said, glancing around the room. 'Where is your man, Sir Walter?'

'I sent him to report the theft of my ruby ring, sir.'

'And what is his name?'

'John Sturley.'

'I must speak with John Sturley. He may well have something to tell me which will be of interest to Her Majesty. Where is he?'

'But what of my ring, sir?'

'The queen's life is more important than any bauble. Where is your man now?'

Sir Walter raised his head and pretended to look around the room. 'I... I do not see him, sir.'

Robert Cecil turned to the guards. 'He must be found!' he ordered. 'Have the palace searched for him!'

The guests were quite panic-stricken as the guards pushed their way amongst them, barking out John Sturley's name.

I tried to catch Robert Cecil's attention 'Pardon me, sir.'

'What is it, boy?' he snapped.

'The apothecary that sold the poison – will you arrest him too? He is likely to leave London once he hears Sir Walter is under suspicion.'

'Where is this apothecary's shop?' Robert Cecil asked.

'In an alley off Cheapside,' Alice replied.

'Then you can show the way. I'll send some guards with you.'

We both nodded, excited at the thought of seeing Gideon de Laine arrested.

Robert Cecil snapped his fingers and a guard scurried forward, head bowed, waiting for instructions.

'Sergeant, take some men and two wherries down the river to the city,' he commanded. 'These youths will take you to an apothecary by the name of Gideon de Laine. Arrest him. He will tell us the truth once he sees the rack.'

Mother Trowte was excited to hear it. 'A bit of torture, that's what he needs, Master Cecil,' she said. 'I'll go with 'em to make sure he gets there.' And she bobbed a curtsey as well as her bad knees would allow.

'No, madam,' he replied. 'You are too old to run around the streets of London in this weather. Stay here and look after these two lively young boys.'

Mother Trowte looked disappointed, and Willum and Jack whined and complained at being left out – but nobody listened.

The sergeant did not look pleased, either. He stared at Alice and me like we had crawled out of a dung heap. 'You want these children to lead my men, sir?' he said. 'Surely not.'

'Go!' Robert Cecil bellowed, 'Go at once.' And the guard clicked his heels and spun round, marching towards the door with Alice and me following behind.

We were given cloaks to wrap around us against the cold and we left the Palace attended by eight yeoman guards. By then the snow was several inches deep and when we reached the banks of the Thames we found watermen sitting shivering in their wherries, waiting for their next customer with their caps pulled over their ears.

The sergeant called to them and the watermen leaped onto the shore and came running. 'This is the queen's business,' the sergeant barked. 'I need to get to Paul's Stairs in double-quick time. Who is the fastest?'

Hands shot up.

'Take my boat,' said one.

'Mine is faster,' said another.

'I shall take yours, Master Waterman,' the sergeant called to the nearest. 'And yours,' he said, pointing to the next. 'You will be paid well.'

In each wherry there were two watermen with powerful hands and strong, muscular arms. As soon as we had climbed on board, they dipped their long oars into the Thames and moved off, the boats skimming over the water and gathering speed. The watermen bent forward and back...forward and back...pulling on their oars without pausing. But, as the boats moved faster, the icy air whipped at our faces so that we began to shiver and could not stop.

The wherries sped past Blackfriars Stairs and on along the

river until we saw the dark silhouette of Baynard's Castle on the shore. On we went, and soon after we reached the foot of Paul's Stairs and the boats were pulled up.

In an attempt to stand, we gripped the side of the wherry. But it was rocking on the water and bumping against the shore, making it impossible to climb out. Not only that, we were hampered by our long frocks which tangled around our legs.

The watermen laughed at our predicament. 'It ain't easy, is it?' one called. 'Come on, I'll help you.' And he leaned over and picked up Alice and me as if we were feather pillows. 'Now, you be careful on them stairs,' he said as he dumped us onto the quayside. 'They're slippery with this snow.'

We thanked him and turned towards the flight of stone steps that led up to the city. But in the dark it was impossible to see.

The sergeant shouted to one of the guards ahead of him. 'Call for the linkmen, Harry! We'll need light if we are to find our way.'

We heard him yell, 'Linkmen!' several times, and soon four of them arrived running with torches blazing.

The flames from the torches lit up the steps as we climbed, though we had to take care not to trip on our skirts. Once we had reached the top, the sergeant pointed at me. 'You!' he snapped. 'What's your name?'

'I am Thomas, sir.'

'Well, Thomas, which way to this apothecary?'

'I know,' Alice butted in. 'Straight ahead, sir.'

The guard nodded. 'Run as fast as you can and my men will follow. Robert Cecil won't be pleased if we don't catch that rogue.'

We raced alongside the linkmen, slipping and sliding in the snow with the wind snapping at our noses and the wet seeping through our thin shoes. When we reached Bread Street Alice shouted, 'Straight ahead over Cheapside. Carry on until we reach Milk Street.'

We ran on and were halfway up Milk Street and about to turn into the close where the apothecary lived when a tall man, wrapped in a dark cloak, came dashing past.

'Out of my way!' he shouted, pushing Alice aside, sending her tumbling into the snow.

'Oy!' she shouted, grabbing hold of his cloak. 'Watch it, mister!' Then, as the cloak fell away, light from the torches shone on his face revealing a crooked eye and a scarred cheek.

'It's John Sturley!' I yelled as the man set off running. 'Quick! Stop him!'

Although I chased after him I knew I wouldn't catch him for his stride was much longer than mine. Then something came hurtling through the air and struck him on the head. *Bang!* It was a snowball hurled by Alice and hard as a cannonball. The shock of it made him lose his balance and sent him slithering about until he fell, bawling and yelling, into a pile of slush.

Two guards were on him straight away and dragged him to his feet as Alice and I ran up from behind.

'So, this is John Sturley, is it?' the sergeant asked me.

'Yes,' I panted. 'Sir Walter Loddington's man.'

'That's him, all right,' said Alice, pausing to get her breath back. 'Him and his master, Sir Walter Loddington, are plotting to kill the queen, they are.'

'Then he's heading for the hangman's rope.'

'Lies!' yelled John Sturley as he struggled to free himself from the guard's grip. 'Do you believe these…these… urchins? They are nothing!'

The sergeant pulled a long strip of leather from his pocket. 'Is that so?' he said, narrowing his eyes. 'But Master Secretary Cecil don't think they're nothing and I do *his* bidding not yours.'

Sturley cursed but the sergeant ignored his prisoner's foul language and bound his hands together so tightly that he screamed.

Alice was soaked after her fall but that didn't stop her confronting Sturley. She stepped up close to him, her fingers bunched into angry fists. 'Been to see the apothecary, have you? Told him to get out of London quick, eh? Well, just wait till the guards take him before our queen. She'll make him talk, see if she don't! You'll lose your head – and good riddance too.'

To my surprise, John Sturley's face twisted into an evil smile. 'Take me to Her Majesty, if you will. I have nothing to hide. You have no proof of a poisoning and you will find nothing to condemn me nor my master.'

I couldn't help wondering why he was so confident. He had been accused of buying poison. He might be tortured or hanged. Most men would have turned to jelly at the thought of it. Why was he smiling?

It was then that my nose twitched and I smelled something. I glanced up Milk Street and my nose twitched again. Now I recognised the stench of burning and it was coming from the close where the apothecary lived.

Chapter 33

Bridging the Gap

'Fire!' I yelled. 'Come on!'

We raced round the corner into a wall of thick, black smoke which filled our lungs and set us coughing and choking.

I tried to call, 'Fire!' again, but before I could, there was an explosion and a fireball burst through a downstairs window.

'It's the apothecary's shop!' Alice shouted as we backed away, shielding our faces from the heat and the bright light.

Doors and windows in the close were flung open and people looked out to see what was happening.

'Fire!' I shouted, and neighbours rushed from their houses carrying buckets and ran to fetch water from the nearest fountain at Saint Mary le Bow. Others scooped up snow and flung it at the flames like some frantic game of snowballs. A few, who were afraid for their own homes, hurried past with boxes and bedding and anything they could carry.

The guards followed us to the close, two of them dragging John Sturley.

'He started the fire!' Alice screamed as she pointed at him. 'He did it!'

Sturley laughed a nasty mocking laugh and shook his head. 'What proof do you have? What proof is a pile of ashes and a dead man?'

But no sooner had he spoken than the window over the shop swung open. We all looked up and saw a head topped with a black cap poke out.

'It's the apothecary,' cried Alice. 'He ain't dead!'

'Let him die!' shouted John Sturley. 'He was the one who plotted to poison the queen not my master.' But the guards took no notice. They flung him to the ground and bound his feet so that he couldn't escape.

Meanwhile, the apothecary hung out of the window like a ragdoll. 'Save me!' he croaked.

'We need a ladder to reach him,' the sergeant called to his men. 'You two. Come with me to the church.' And they ran after him into Milk Street.

Alice was furious. 'A ladder ain't going to do no good, is it? By the time they get back, the old devil will be burned to a cinder.'

To prove her point the apothecary groaned and slithered out of sight, unable to hold onto the windowsill.

'Oh, gawd, Thomas. Now he'll never go before the queen. Our proof's gone for certain.'

But I hadn't given up yet. 'The gap is narrow from his window to the one across the alley,' I said, nodding at the house opposite. 'I think I can get across.'

The people from that building had fled with their belongings, leaving their front door open. We ran in and climbed up to the bedchamber which overhung the close.

'We'll bridge the gap between this room and the apothecary's,' I said, standing at the window.

'How can you, Thomas?'

I looked around the room and spotted a narrow truckle bed in the corner. 'This will do,' I said, and we pulled off the mattress and carried the wooden base to the window.

'It won't go through,' puffed Alice. 'The bed's too wide.'

'Not much. We'll use it as a battering ram and make the opening bigger.'

Together we carried the truckle bed back to the wall and then we charged like a rampaging army with a battering ram, smashing the window frame, and showering glass and shards of wood onto the people below.

'Vandals!' they shouted up at us and shook their fists.

'The queen will pay,' I called down as we pushed the bed through the hole and across the gap until it rested on the apothecary's windowsill.

All I had to do was cross it.

'Careful, Thomas,' said Alice. 'It's a long way down. Don't you go falling.'

I leaned out, spread myself full length on the wooden bed and began to wriggle along, feeling confident. I would have been as right as rain if I hadn't looked down. I shouldn't have done it but I couldn't help myself. As I stared at the long drop below me, my head began to spin and my stomach churned. I shut my eyes and gripped the bed tight, my fingers curling round the edge, clinging on. One slip, I thought, and that would be the end of me.

But by the time I had reached halfway, there was a danger far worse than the drop. Smoke was billowing up from the door of the apothecary's shop. It was so thick and black that it filled my mouth and blocked my nose, making me choke. I could do nothing except cough and gasp for air. My eyes were streaming so badly that I couldn't see. Although I tried spitting out the filthy stuff, it made no difference. I couldn't breathe.

The neighbours standing below were shouting. 'Don't move, lad. Wait for the ladder. It will be here soon.'

I clung on, choking and retching, fearing I would die for lack of good clean air. I would never see my family again. I would never be a rich and famous actor. I was doomed.

Then a miracle happened. Quite suddenly, the wind changed direction taking the smoke away down the close so that, at last, I could breathe again.

I wiped my eyes and began to move forward along the truckle bed inch by inch until my fingers finally gripped the sill and I dragged myself into the apothecary's room. More smoke inside. This time rising through the floorboards. It was impossible to see, and as I felt my way I stumbled and fell, landing on something soft. Something warm. It was the body of Gideon de Laine. I reached out and felt his greasy beard and wrinkled skin and my fingers felt his open mouth.

With a shudder, I rolled off him and kneeled on the floor, grasping hold of his shoulders and shaking him to see if he was dead or alive.

'Master Apothecary,' I said. No reply. 'Master Apothecary,' I repeated and shook him harder.

At that moment, a piece of floorboard caught fire throwing light upon his face. *He's dead*, I thought, and I leaned closer, putting my hand near to his nostrils to feel for any breath. It was then that his eyes suddenly shot open and he raised his head.

I gasped and snatched away my hand. I tried to stay calm, though I felt all of a tremble. 'We need to go now,' I said. 'Can you stand?'

He gripped my arm with his bony fingers and, without a word, he sat coughing and spluttering. With a great effort, I pulled him to his feet and draped his arm across my shoulder.

'The bottle,' he gasped, pointing to the bench. 'Give it to me.'

Without thinking, I put the bottle in his hand and he drank half the contents before coughing violently then drinking the rest. It seemed to calm him, but I was anxious to get out of the building.

'The fire is coming up the stairs,' I said, supporting him as best I could. 'We must get out.'

'I know about the fire,' he growled. 'I know.'

Then suddenly he shook himself free of me as if he had found his strength again. Whatever potion he had taken had aided his recovery miraculously. One minute he had been near to death and now he was at the window climbing onto the sill. But when the pocket of his robe caught on a nail, he was held back. 'Damn you!' he cursed and tugged at it so violently that the fabric ripped. Then he scrambled out and kneeled on the wooden bed that bridged the gap between the houses.

One of the guards watching below called, 'Careful, old man.' But Gideon de Laine did not hesitate, determined to escape the fire. He crawled across like an antiquated baby until he reached the other side and dropped into the room where Alice was waiting. I knew he would recognise her straight away. She would think he must be weak from the smoke. But I knew he was not.

'Take care!' I shouted across to my friend. 'Get help!'

But it was too late. The old devil swiped his hand across her face with such force that he knocked her sideways, sending her reeling backwards onto the floor.

'Stop it!' I shouted as I climbed onto the windowsill ready to go and help her. But Gideon de Laine would have his revenge on me too. He turned and lifted the end of the bed, pushing it out of the window and sending it crashing down into the alley. There was no way across.

I turned back from the window thinking I might try the stairs when I saw something on the floor. Just below the window, was the apothecary's black book. It must have fallen from his pocket when his robe caught on the nail. My heart leaped. I snatched up the book and opened it. It was the account book Jack had found. Now we had proof. We could take it to the queen. But, as I held it in my hand, flames reached the top of the stairs and burst into the room. Everything around me began to catch fire.

Chapter 34
Like an Old Worm

The smoke was making me choke and tears were running down my cheeks so that I couldn't see. Desperately I hung out of the window and, when I heard the guards running towards me, I prayed that they would reach me in time.

'We'll soon have you down!' they shouted. 'We've got the ladder.' And they leaned it against the wall.

I could scarcely breathe. Would the flames hold back for a few seconds? But my head was already spinning and my legs could barely hold me. I held on as long as I could, and as I began to fall strong hands grabbed hold of me and I was tossed over someone's shoulder like a sack of turnips.

'Hold onto me, lad!' the guard shouted. But it's not easy to hold on when you are hanging upside down. Being carried down a ladder dressed as a girl, it's not something a boy would want to do.

Once my feet were on the ground I stood in the snow, coughing and shivering with cold, until I heard Alice's voice.

'The old goat!' she bawled and I turned to see her stomping out of the house opposite – alive and well but in a very bad temper. 'He punched me! Well, I showed him, didn't I?'

I gasped. 'But I saw him knock you down.'

She stood in front of me, her hands on her hips. 'You didn't think he'd done for me, did you, Thomas?' she said.

'Well, he hadn't. While he was shoving that bed through the window, I hit him with a candlestick and knocked the lights out of him.' She clapped her hand across her mouth and started to giggle. 'It was a real jest.'

'Then what happened?'

'I flung the mattress over him and I sat on him. And when them guards came upstairs, they says, "What's going on? Where's that apothecary?" And there he was under the mattress squiggling around like an old worm and me sitting on top of him.' Alice stood rocking with laughter and when she saw the guards drag Gideon de Laine out of the house, she laughed even more.

The alleyway was crowded by then. Word of the fire had reached Milk Street and Cheapside, and people had come with their buckets. They formed a chain, passing them from hand to hand, bringing water from the nearby fountain.

They managed to put it out before it spread. By then, we were well on the way to Whitehall Palace. We had to face Her Majesty prove that Sir Walter Loddington was a poisoner and that Master Shakespeare was no thief.

Chapter 35

Emerald Earrings

When we reached Whitehall Palace three of the guards marched John Sturley and Gideon de Laine down to the cells. Master Tilney was waiting for us looking very stern indeed, 'Follow me,' he said. 'Her Majesty expects you in the presence chamber.'

Alice nudged me. 'What's the presence chamber?' she whispered.

I shrugged. 'I suppose it's just another room. There must be hundreds of 'em.'

We trudged down long corridors, our wet skirts dragging on the floorboards, our shoes squelching with snow, until we came to a huge door where Master Tilney stopped and turned to face us.

'Her Majesty is waiting for you,' he said solemnly. 'She has members of the privy council with her. Be careful of your manners.'

I didn't know what a privy council was, but it sounded scary and I thought it must be of great significance.

Master Tilney opened the door and stepped into a large room with a high ceiling painted gold. At the far end, sitting on a large throne-like chair, was the queen herself. She was surrounded by important-looking men in fine clothes with ruffs around their necks and frowns on their faces. One of them was Robert Cecil. But best of all Master Shakespeare was there looking quite cheerful.

Master Tilney strode across the room side by side with the yeoman. Alice and I scuttled behind them feeling as nervous as kittens in a dog kennel.

'Your Majesty,' said Master Tilney, bowing before the queen. 'The mission was successful. The apothecary and John Sturley have been taken to the cells and are now alongside Sir Walter Loddington.'

''Tis well done,' said the queen. 'And what of these young people? Why are they here, Master Tilney?'

Robert Cecil stepped forward. 'Your Majesty,' he replied, 'I requested they should be brought before you for they know more about the apothecary and the poison plot than anyone else.'

The queen tapped her fingers on her lips. 'Indeed, Master Secretary?' She held her head high and looked down at us. 'And what are your names?'

We bowed our heads. 'I am Thomas, Your Majesty.'

'And my name is ... er ... Barnaby,' said Alice, almost forgetting what she should say.

'Then you are the youths who brought this tale of treason to our attention,' the queen said. 'We have listened to what Master Shakespeare had to say, and I have discussed the activities of Gideon de Laine with my councillors. It seems that indeed we do have a traitor in our midst.' She flapped her hand at us. 'I wish you to wait here. We may need to ask questions of you.'

Then she turned to speak to her privy council. 'Gentlemen, we must uphold the law of the land. First we must see what those evil men have to say for themselves.' She beckoned to the sergeant. 'Bring the men from the cells at once. The traitors must be punished.'

While we waited for the prisoners to arrive, I took a deep breath and stepped forward to speak to the queen. 'If it pleases Your Majesty,' I said, bowing low and nervously holding out the black book.

'What is this, boy?' she asked without taking it from me.

'It belonged to the apothecary, Your Majesty,' I said, standing upright. Then I opened it at the page dated the twenty-fourth of November and presented it. 'If Your Majesty would look at this I think you will find it of interest.'

She took the book. I bowed again and stepped away.

Squeezing her eyes so she could see better, she read the page. 'Interesting indeed,' she said, before handing the book to Sir Robert Cecil who was standing close to her chair. He read it quickly and passed it on to the councillor next to him.

By the time every privy councillor had seen the book, Sir Walter Loddington had been brought up from the cells. He was a frightened man, and when he was made to stand before the queen he trembled, not daring to raise his eyes from the floor.

John Sturley was next, his hands bound, his face swollen and bruised from the beating the guards had given him. He was dragged into the room, struggling and sobbing, and was placed next to his master.

The last to arrive was Gideon de Laine, growling like a tethered bear. Out of the three of them, only he seemed unafraid. He was placed on the other side of Sir Walter, and although his face was smoke-blackened from the fire, he still held his chin high.

The queen rose out of her chair and stood before them, stiff-backed and silent but staring at the three men with cold loathing. When she did speak there was ice in her voice.

'You are all accused of involvement in a most heinous crime – that of attempting to poison our royal personage. What say you?'

No one spoke.

'What? Have you lost your tongues!' she roared. 'Have you no honour? What shame have you brought upon yourselves?'

At last, they spoke.

One by one they denied plotting to kill her.

One by one they declared their loyalty to the crown.

Of the three of them only Gideon de Laine's voice rang strong, without a tremble.

Then Alice stepped forward and curtseyed low to the queen. 'If it pleases Your Majesty,' she said. 'I heard the apothecary tell Master Sturley to put the poison on some earrings. That's what he said.'

The queen raised her eyebrows and nodded as if what Alice had said made sense. Then she turned to address Sir Walter. 'You gave me a present at the Christmas festivities, did you not?' she asked. 'A pair of emerald earrings?'

I saw his hands begin to shake and he linked his fingers together to try to control them. But they shook all the more. 'I…Er…Y-yes, Y-Your Majesty,' he stammered. 'And… Er…You seemed d-d-delighted with the gift.'

'Perhaps it was fortunate that I did not wear them,' replied the queen. 'I was once given a poisoned dress, you know, and I escaped death that time too.'

'Majesty,' interrupted Sir Walter. 'There w-was no plot to poison you. I b-beg you…'

She waved a regal hand at him as if swatting away a fly and then she picked up the black book, opened it at the twenty-fourth of November and ran her finger down the items listed. 'Perhaps your man will explain why you were in the apothecary's shop and why Master De Laine was paid so many gold coins? Tell me, John Sturley.'

Sturley did not dare reply. But when the queen grew tired of waiting she shouted in a most un-queen-like way, 'You will answer, Master Sturley. Or would you rather be stretched on the rack? They say it takes no time at all before bones crack.'

When he heard that Sturley fell to his knees. 'I beg you, Your Majesty, I was not a part of any plot. I am only a servant. It was the apothecary who sold the poison and the gold was Sir Walter's. I am innocent.'

Queen Elizabeth turned to Alice. 'And you were working for the apothecary, were you, Barnaby? You saw all this?'

Alice nodded. 'I did, Your Majesty. I saw these men come and buy the poison. The apothecary sold it and told him how to use it.'

The queen kept the book in her hand and nodded before turning to Gideon de Laine. 'What do you say to that, apothecary? Did you sell poison to Sir Walter?'

Gideon de Laine stood proud and surprisingly calm. 'Lies, Your Majesty. I cure people, I do not poison them. But sometimes my potions come at a high price,' he explained, pointing towards the black book.

The queen smiled. 'You seem to be a learned man, I must say, and I am glad of your explanation.' Then she turned away and faced Sir Walter Loddington. 'This servant of yours,' she said, waving her hand towards John Sturley, who was still cowering on his knees, 'does he tell falsehoods?'

'Indeed he does, Your Majesty, for I never bought any such potion. I intend to punish him most severely and I shall dismiss him from my service.'

The queen nodded again and went to sit in her chair, smoothing her skirt as if the matter had come to an end.

'Then let us be friends,' she said, smiling. 'And to show you how pleased I am with your gift, Sir Walter, I shall send for the emerald earrings and put them on.' She beckoned a servant standing close by. 'Fetch the earrings in the little black box,' she said and he left the room immediately returning shortly with a velvet casket which he presented to her.

But the queen did not take it. Instead, she waved it away. 'Let us see my loyal friend try the earrings, shall we?' There was a buzz of excitement as everyone stared at Sir Walter.

'As you know,' the queen continued, 'I never wear anything or eat anything unless it is tested first.' She paused, fixing her eyes on him. 'Oh, you did not know that, Sir Walter?' she asked, clapping her hands and smiling as if it was all a game. 'I think that is why I have lived so long, don't you?' Then, quite suddenly, she narrowed her eyes and her voice grew sharper. 'Pick up the earrings, sir, and put them to your ears,' she commanded.

Sir Walter's face turned grey and he trembled like an old man with the palsy. He raised a shaking hand as if to open the casket. 'I . . . c-cannot . . .' he stammered, and withdrew it before he broke down, sobbing.

'Well, Sir Walter,' she rasped. 'I see that you are both a liar and fool. Now, tell me, was the apothecary lying too?'

'He was, Your Majesty,' he said, recovering his speech and pointing accusingly at Gideon de Laine. 'He made the poison. It is said that he is from Spain, Your Majesty, and is in league with King Philip who would take your throne if he could.'

The apothecary, raging with anger, suddenly leaped forward at Sir Walter Loddington like a tiger at its prey, but the guards were quick to grab him and he was pulled back.

'This is treason!' the queen bellowed. 'You are traitors, all three of you, and you shall have a traitor's death in due course. What say you, gentlemen?' she asked her privy councillors.

They muttered among themselves before declaring their decision. 'If it is proved, Your Majesty, then indeed they should suffer a traitor's death. Hanging, drawing and quartering as the law allows.'

The queen, satisfied with their pronouncement, turned next to Master Shakespeare. 'These men involved you in their lies, did they not?' she said. 'I do not believe you stole the ring, for you are no thief.'

Master Shakespeare stepped forward and bowed low. 'Indeed no, Your Majesty. I have no call to play the robber.'

'Quite so,' said the queen. 'When the ring was not found on you, I believe John Sturley insisted you had passed it on to one of your troupe.'

'It was a trick so that Sir Walter could hold my actors at the palace. I believe his plan was to take Barnaby. He had already tried to kill him at the apothecary's shop.'

'So Barnaby would not be able to tell me of their vile plot.'

Master Shakespeare bowed his head. 'That is so, Your Majesty.'

'Then we shall speak no more of these lies,' she said. 'You shall write more plays and entertain your queen as you always have.' She waved towards the guards. 'Take the traitors out of my sight.'

Two yeomen grasped Sir Walter Loddington by the arm. Two more took hold of John Sturley and they were both dragged away, protesting. As Gideon de Laine was taken he glowered at Master Shakespeare, his face convulsed with so much spite that my spine ran cold with fear.

'Think not that you are safe,' he growled. 'For I will take you with me to the executioner.'

Everyone gasped, wondering what he meant. Then, as the guards marched him across the room, he bellowed, 'You have been fooled, Your Majesty. The apprentice Barnaby is no boy. Master Shakespeare has broken the laws of England.'

The room grew silent and every eye was turned on Alice while the apothecary's laugh could be heard as he was dragged through the door and down below to the dungeons.

Chapter 36

A Slippery Eel

The queen gripped the arm of her chair, shocked by what she had heard. 'A girl? Performing in my palace? A girl? Is this so?'

Quaking, Alice stepped forward – very bravely I thought. 'If it pleases Your Majesty,' she said, with her head bent low, 'it were no fault of Master Shakespeare's.'

The queen sank back in her chair and closed her eyes to shut out the sight of those standing in front of her. The room was silent. You could have heard a pin drop. Then she opened her eyes and spoke in a low voice. 'Master Shakespeare has broken my laws and will be punished – and so will you.' She glanced across at the guards. 'Take them to the Tower.'

The privy councillors looked grave but no one spoke a word of protest as the two of them were led towards the door. Alice was small and skinny she wriggled out of their grasp like a slippery eel and ran back to the queen.

'That ain't fair,' Alice sobbed, standing three paces from her. 'He didn't know I was a girl when he took me in, Your Majesty. I was in terrible danger from that apothecary. Out to murder me, he was.' Alice paused to wipe her cheeks. 'I used to love them stories my ma used to tell me about kings and queens. There was one I remember about you when you was a princess. You was in danger just like me, wasn't you?'

227

The privy councillors gasped at Alice's words. Nobody dared speak in such a familiar way to the ruler of England – not if they valued their head.

The guards gripped Alice's arms once more, and waited for the queen's instructions. I expected her to burst into a torrent of poisonous words and send Alice to the hangman. But she did not. Perhaps Alice had reminded her of her own childhood when her mother, Anne Boleyn, was beheaded and King Henry wanted nothing to do with his daughter.

Nobody moved. Then, slowly, ever so slowly, Her Majesty rose from her seat. She stood for a moment looking down at the defiant Alice before she turned her back on us and faced the wall. Still nobody dared to move. It seemed ages and ages until, at last, the queen spun round, her eyes sweeping the room, daring any of us to make a sound. Then, looking straight at the guards, she spoke – her voice almost a whisper. 'Release them. I should like to question them further.'

The sergeant bowed his head, the guards let go of Alice and Master Shakespeare and marched back across the room to their positions by the door.

'Now, tell me,' said the queen, narrowing her eyes and fixing them on Alice. 'Explain how you came to break the law.' She lowered herself into her chair once again and leaned back, ready to listen.

Alice sniffed and wiped her nose with the back of her hand. She told the queen how she had run away from the cruel landlord of the Black Boar at Uxbridge and travelled to London with me. And how she had tried to earn money for her family who were very poor and lived by Cripplegate, and how she had been cruelly treated by the three men who had been brought before the queen.

'If all that is true, it is a terrible story indeed,' said the queen. 'Nevertheless, you have deceived me and contradicted the laws of England for which there are severe punishments. Is that not so, Master Secretary?'

Robert Cecil nodded. 'Indeed it is so, Your Majesty,' he said with great relish. 'But there is also the involvement of Master Shakespeare. He must suffer punishment too, for he employed the girl.' Everybody held their breath, waiting for more. He would be sure to find punishments for as many people as possible. 'In addition,' he commanded, 'the right of the Chamberlain's Men to perform must be taken away immediately.'

There was a great deal of muttering and nodding, and Alice hung her head as the queen turned to Master Shakespeare.

'Come,' she said. 'Step forward and speak your piece.'

Master Shakespeare didn't hesitate. He flung himself on his knees in front of her.

'I am your most loyal servant, Your Majesty,' he said, his voice quivering like a leaf in a gale. 'It was never my intention to deceive you.'

The queen stood again, frowning and not replying to his words. Instead, she paced the floor, four paces this way, four paces that. All eyes were on her until, eventually, she stopped and said, 'Master Shakespeare, I have given this some consideration. You have broken the law most seriously.'

At those words, I turned cold as the snow on the palace roof. If Alice and Master Shakespeare were sent to the Tower it would be my fault. I had taken Alice to the Curtain. I had deceived Master Shakespeare into thinking she was a boy. I closed my eyes, ashamed and sick with fear.

'I believe,' the queen said as she brushed an imaginary speck of dust from her sleeve. 'I believe, Master Shakespeare, that you were not aware that this child was a girl.' Then she looked at him. 'As deceit was not your intention,' she paused and coughed politely, 'we shall therefore pardon you.'

I felt a surge of relief. I could hardly believe it. But it was true. He was free! I felt like jumping for joy and flinging my arms in the air and yelling 'Hurray!' a hundred times.

Master Shakespeare struggled to his feet. 'I am grateful to Your Majesty,' he said, sweeping his arm across his chest and bowing low. 'If you will allow me, I shall write a play dedicated to my queen. I am to build a new playhouse south of the river, and I promise that the new play will be performed at the opening. I would be honoured ... deeply honoured ... if you would attend.'

She threw back her head and laughed so hard that the white make-up on her face cracked into a web of lines that made her look a hundred years old – but I don't suppose she realised.

'A playhouse outside the city walls?' she mocked. 'Why, Master Shakespeare, I should never attend such a place. They are a den of thieves and cut-throats.'

Nevertheless, the queen seemed pleased with his invitation and gave one of her black-toothed smiles.

Maybe she'll be just as kind to Alice, I thought.

When Alice was summoned, she was all of a tremble and flopped onto her knees, just like Master Shakespeare had done.

The queen stared down at her. 'You have deceived me,' she said in a disappointed voice. 'You are a maid, and by acting on the stage you have dared to defy me. This is the very worst kind of deception. I am your sovereign lady and I command loyalty.' She paused before leaning forward and lifting Alice's chin so that she looked her full in the face. 'But you and your friend Thomas have saved my life this day and therefore I shall pardon you.'

Alice's mouth fell open. 'Oh, Your Majesty,' she gasped. 'Thank you. You have been merciful indeed, Your Majesty. And there I was, thinking—'

The queen held up her hand for silence. 'You have suffered much in the hands of Gideon de Laine,' she said. 'It seems that you have saved me from yet another conspiracy by the Spanish who doubtless paid Sir Walter well to poison me.' She placed her hand on Alice's shoulder. 'As a token of my gratitude I shall ask Robert Cecil to find a house for you so that your family may live in comfort.' Then she paused and frowned. 'But as for your acting, I look harshly upon it. I forbid you ever to walk onto a stage again. It is not seemly for a young maid.'

So the day ended with three evil men imprisoned in the Tower while Master Shakespeare and Alice were given a royal pardon.

Chapter 37

A Disappearing Theatre

Alice had to leave the Chamberlain's Men, of course, but she was happy enough to return to her family, who soon moved into a neat house off Candlewick Street, which was the queen's reward for bringing the traitors to justice.

As for Master Shakespeare, he was determined to build a new playhouse. He had bought some land in rough area near the Clink Prison where you had to watch out for stews and footpads and all manner of rogues who would slit your throat as soon as look at you. But before he could start to build it he needed plenty of timber, and in pursuit of this, he hatched a plan.

One freezing cold night just after Christmas, he persuaded a dozen friends and members of the Chamberlain's men (including me) to go with him to demolish a playhouse called the Theatre and remove the timber. Although the land the Theatre stood on belonged to Giles Allen, Master Shakespeare was certain that he had paid for all the oak used in the building itself. The two men had quarrelled about it for years.

We all agreed to help him pull down the Theatre while Giles Allen was away visiting his family for Christmas. We must have looked a strange sight that night as we marched through Shoreditch in falling snow carrying axes and bill-hooks to do the job. But, in just a few hours, we had knocked down the playhouse and loaded the timbers onto carts. It was bitterly cold — so cold that the Thames was frozen solid. Somehow we got the wood to the other side of the river before the landlord came back to Shoreditch.

When Giles Allen found out what had happened they say he turned purple with rage. But it was too late. The Theatre was gone and Master Shakespeare had already started to build his new playhouse.

Some weeks later the Chamberlain's Men were gathered at the White Swan discussing our future in the new theatre.

'How many people will it hold, Will?' Richard Burbage asked.

Master Shakespeare grinned. 'How many? An amazing number,' he roared, raising his tankard high. 'The audience could be a thousand. No! Two thousand. Maybe three!'

We all shouted, 'Marvellous!' 'Astonishing!' 'The biggest ever!' and banged our tankards on the table.

Then Master Kemp asked, 'But shall it have a stage good enough for my dances?'

'I promise you,' said Master Shakespeare, taking a swallow of his ale, 'my theatre will be as round as an O and will have the grandest stage, with the finest roof made of the best thatch.' He stood up and spread his arms wide. 'It will be the most magnificent theatre in the land. Nay, in the whole world.'

We all raised our tankards and cheered loud enough to lift the roof off the tavern.

'And do you have you a name for this fine theatre, Will?' asked Richard Burbage.

'Not yet. But let me think on it.' The great man paused, looking up to the ceiling for inspiration, chewing on his ink-stained fingers before he said, 'I shall call it the Fortune.'

'No,' Master Kemp replied. 'There's a playhouse of that name already.'

'The Swan?'

'Nay, Will. There is one not far from here.'

Master Shakespeare went into a sulk. 'Well, you think of something then,' he snapped and turned his back on us.

We all fell silent, glancing at each other, not able to come up with any names that seemed suitable.

Trying to be helpful, I said, 'If the theatre is to be the best in the world, sir, you could call it the World.'

But nobody thought that was very good and I was given a punch on the shoulder for my trouble. No one else said a word.

I bit on my thumbnail and thought some more until an image came into my head. 'What do you call one of those round things, sir?' I asked.

'What round things?' Master Shakespeare asked without much interest.

'I mean one of those round things with the world painted on it?'

He sniffed and looked bored. 'That is a globe, boy,' he muttered and took another mouthful of ale.

'Then, if your theatre is to be the finest in the world, sir,' I said, 'why not call it the Globe?'

He almost choked on his beer as he spun, a smile spread

across his face and his eyes lit up, all of a sparkle. 'The Globe!' he cried, slapping his palm on the table. 'That's it! Excellent, Thomas! Excellent! Yes, the Globe it shall be. And I shall have a flag made to fly above the theatre when we perform and it shall show Hercules carrying the world on his back. It will be magnificent!' He raised his tankard again. 'Are we agreed, men?'

There was an explosion of cheering and laughing and back-slapping. It was the perfect name for our wonderful new playhouse. And was even more special to me because I had thought of it.

It was planned that the Globe should open in the summer with the new play which Master Shakespeare had promised the queen. It was called *Julius Caesar*.

'Who's Julius Caesar?' asked Alice one day when she came to visit.

'He's a sort of roman king – but they didn't call them kings in Rome,' I explained. 'The play's about quarrels between the rulers years and years ago.'

'Sounds boring.'

'No! There are murders in it and stabbings and plenty of blood.'

'Well,' said Alice, laughing. 'It makes a change from poisoned earrings.'

'Will your mother come to the opening?'

'Course she will! We'll all come,' said Alice. 'We wouldn't miss it for the world.'

By summer that year the building was nearly done, and Master Shakespeare came to speak to me. 'You are a fine boy,

Thomas,' he said, patting my shoulder. 'Every day you remind me of my poor son and I am proud of you.'

I felt my cheeks grow pink with embarrassment but I managed to say, 'Thank you, sir.'

'I have a mind,' he continued, 'to invite your family to the opening of the Globe. Do you think they would like to come?'

'Oh yes, sir,' I replied, bursting with excitement. 'I have written to them about the new theatre. Last year, my father was angry that I had run away. But now he seems proud that I am a member of the Chamberlain's Men and performed before the queen.'

'Then it is time he saw what a fine actor you are.'

I was overwhelmed. Master Shakespeare was to send them an invitation! But there were difficulties.

'Sir, how will they get here?'

He held up his hand. 'I shall arrange for a carrier to fetch them. I insist. It is my thanks to them for sending me such an intelligent boy.'

This was a generous offer indeed. I was bubbling with excitement at the thought that Beth and John and Father would see this great city of London. They would see me acting with the Chamberlain's Men. What a surprise that would be.

But would Father come? He had always said he had no wish to travel outside of Stratford. Then I thought if my cousin Richard came, he would look after Beth and John even if Father decided to stay at home.

'Could my cousin come with them, sir?' I asked. 'He is a strong man and I should like to think he would take care of my family on the journey. No vagabond would dare to stop the cart with Richard on board.'

'Of course, Thomas. There'll be room on the cart for another one. I shall write to your father at once.'

That day Master Shakespeare penned a note and sent it off, and I wondered what Father would think when he received a letter with the seal of the great man himself. I dare say he would hardly believe his eyes.

Two weeks later Master Shakespeare received a reply from my family saying that they would be honoured to accept. Hurray! I was going to see them again after many months apart. And, the biggest surprise of all, Father was coming! He sounded so pleased – more like the father he used to be before our mother died.

I could not wait to see him.

Chapter 38
A Grand Opening

That summer my family travelled all the way to London in a cart which Master Shakespeare had paid for – even the hay for the horse – and they were to arrive the day before the grand opening of the Globe.

I had been waiting for them all day, glancing every now and then from an upstairs window. And, when I finally heard the cart pull up outside the lodgings, I ran out to meet them, followed by some of the actors, and together we made a great deal of noise – cheering and laughing and whooping, making passers-by stare.

Master Shakespeare was there and came to greet them too. He bowed low and declared, 'You are most welcome!' as he held out his hand to help Beth down from the cart.

I had almost forgotten what my sister looked like, it had been so long since I left Stratford. She was even prettier than I remembered with her dimpled cheeks and brown eyes and a new yellow dress. Roger, who had washed his face that morning, took a fancy to her right away, and insisted on taking her baggage.

As for John, I hardly recognised my little brother – for he had grown strong and was no longer the pale weakling I had left behind. He leaped off the cart and ran over to me before punching me by way of a brotherly greeting.

'Well, my boy,' Father said, shaking my hand vigorously. 'So this is what happens when you run away to London, is it? You seem to have done well for yourself.' He smiled and his eyes twinkled as they used to when I was little. 'So, all's well that ends well, eh?' he said.

Beth gave me a kiss on the cheek, and cousin Richard gripped my hand and shook it till it almost fell off my arm.

'London is a fine place,' he remarked as we walked down to the White Swan for a plate of pigeon pie. 'Do you know if Sir Walter Raleigh lives here?'

'Everybody lives in London,' I replied.

'They say he found gold in El Dorado,' said Richard. 'Perhaps I shall leave Stratford and Bessy Totthill behind and sail to the New World instead.' He grinned. 'Will you come with me, Thomas?'

I laughed and wondered if he was serious. Would he do such a daring thing as travel to those strange lands where savages lived? If he did, I would not go with him for I had found my place in London.

Once we were settled in the tavern with tasty food inside our bellies Father told me of how life in Stratford had changed since I left.

'Our home is warm and dry, Thomas,' he said. 'For Master Biddle has thatched our roof and replaced the shutters.' He leaned forward and whispered in my ear. 'I think Master Shakespeare had something to do with that.'

Then Beth took my hand, excited to give me her news. 'I no longer take in washing, Thomas,' she said. 'I'm sewing fine linen for the ladies of the town, which pleases me no end. It's good work and I am paid enough to send John to the petty school.'

'I'm learning to read,' said John. 'I will be a scholar, like you, Thomas.'

We all clapped and said what a clever lad he was and, I have to say, I was glad that things were going well for my family.

That evening I took them back to the lodgings where we found room enough for them to sleep and recover from their journey. As for me, I slept little that night for thinking of the following day which promised to be a most exciting one. The next morning broke fair and sunny for the opening of the Globe. All the Chamberlain's Men went early to the theatre and we paced around wondering whether the Globe would be a success. There were butterflies flitting around in my stomach and I worried in case I forgot my lines. And what if the audience didn't like *Julius Caesar* and pelted us with rotten vegetables?

But all turned out well. The opening was a grand affair, with people coming for miles to see the new play. The Trowte family arrived very early and, though Master Shakespeare had seats for them in the balcony, they chose to stand at the front by the stage.

'My eyes ain't so good,' said Mother Trowte, 'I want to see what's going on, I do.'

She was wearing a new black dress for the occasion and a pair of boots that fitted nicely over her bunions. Even the boys looked tidy. 'We combed our hair special,' said Jack while

Willum jumped about showing off his leather shoes. 'Her Majesty sent 'em,' he said. 'She did, honest!'

Alice grinned. 'We've really come to see *you*, Thomas,' she said and winked at me. She was looking pretty as a picture now that her red hair had grown thick and long again.

As for my family, they arrived later, when the theatre was already half full. From backstage I watched them take the seats reserved for them at the front of the balcony under the thatched roof. Father was sitting bolt upright, proud to be in London as Master Shakespeare's guest, knowing that his son was to perform on that fine stage.

We were all ready for the play to begin, standing backstage, wearing our togas which were nothing more than bed sheets. It was hard to think that people in Rome wore such things. Had they never heard of doublet and hose?

Master Shakespeare was pacing about.

'Do you think Her Majesty will come, sir?' I asked him.

He looked at me, tapping the side of his nose. 'She could not come to such a place, Thomas. Too dangerous. Too many rogues and villains.' Then he bent down and whispered in my ear, 'But if she should come in disguise that might be another matter.'

The beating of the drum announced the start of *Julius Caesar*. As we stepped onto the stage the audience fell quiet – all except the Trowtc family who called, 'Thomas!' over and over. Then whistled and shouted, 'Do your bit, Thomas! We're over here!' and waved frantically. But I kept my chin high, pretending not to notice, and looked straight ahead.

As Master Burbage spoke the opening lines, my heart was pumping fit to burst. This was the first performance in the finest playhouse in the land and I was a part of it. The Globe was crammed full of people. Some were standing pressed together in the space in front of the stage, and those folks with more money filled the seats under cover of the roof. There was not a single space left.

While I glanced around, my eye fell on a small lady in the front row of the balcony not far from cousin Richard. There was something familiar about her – the way she held her head, the way she sat straight-backed on the seat. This lady was dressed in black and surrounded by five burly men with swords at their side, who glanced nervously this way and that as if looking for cutthroats. She was the same size as the queen, I thought. She even looked like the queen except that the dress was too plain and she had no pearls around her neck or in her hair.

It was not until the scene when Julius Caesar got stabbed that I knew. It was a very scary part. Terrible screams erupted from Caesar as men lunged forward with daggers and stabbed him in the back so that blood spurted scarlet down his white toga and dripped into pools on the stage.

The lady in the black dress pressed her hand to her mouth, horrified by what she had seen. And that was when I saw her ring. Diamonds and rubies. A special ring. And I knew for sure it was her.

As I ran off the stage at the end of the play I said, 'The queen was in the audience. She was there, up in the balcony! I saw her!'

But nobody believed me. Not Roger nor Master Burbage nor Will Kemp. Not any of the actors.

And when Alice and the Trowte family came round to see me afterwards, I told them. But they didn't believe me, either.

'Her Majesty's an old lady,' said Alice. 'She don't get out much now. It weren't her, Thomas. She'd never come here.'

Even my own family laughed.

'The queen among common folk?' said Richard. 'You are dreaming, coz.'

There was only one person who believed me and that was Master Shakespeare. When I told him who I had seen, he winked and nodded as if to say, *Yes, Thomas. We know, don't we?*

Acknowledgements

Although there is little documented evidence of Shakespeare's life, there have been many books written about him. I am grateful for the scholarship in the books I have consulted, some of which I list below:

Southworth, John 2000, *Shakespeare the Player,* Sutton, London.

Bate, Jonathon 2008, *Soul of the Age,* Viking, London.

Shapiro, James 2003, *1599,* Faber and Faber, London.

Greer, Germaine 2007, *Shakespeare's Wife,* Bloomsbury, London.

Bryson, Bill 2007, *Shakespeare,* Harper Collins, London.

Nicholl, Charles 2008, *The Lodger, Shakespeare on Silver Street,* Penguin, London.

Picard, Liza 2003, *Elizabeth's London,* Orion, London.

Weir, Alison 1998, *Elizabeth the Queen,* Jonathan Cape, London.

Run Rabbit Run

BARBARA MITCHELHILL

When Lizzie's dad refuses to fight in the Second World War, the police come looking to arrest him. Desperate to stay together, Lizzie and her brother Freddie go on the run with him, hiding from the police in idyllic Whiteway. But when their past catches up with them, they're forced to leave and it becomes more and more difficult to stay together as a family. Will they be able to? And will they ever find a place, like Whiteway, where they will be safe again?

Nominated for the Carnegie Medal

'A well-told story showing that bravery comes in many guises.'
Carousel

9781849392495 £5.99

DANGEROUS DIAMONDS

Barbara Mitchelhill

When Dad goes missing, twins Harry and Charlie scour Edinburgh to find him. But why are others determined to stop them? And how is a strange wooden box linked to his disappearance? The twins soon find they are in terrible danger but push themselves to the limit in their attempt to outwit those who are holding their father.

'An adventure thriller full of strong characters and deceit, this book enthralls the reader from the very beginning.'
School Librarian

9781842709788 £4.99

STORM RUNNERS

BARBARA MITCHELHILL

When dramatic storms batter a small Scottish
island and reduce a village to ruins, Ally and
Kirstie think that they are the only survivors.
But then they meet Brad, the son of American
scientists, and together they uncover the terrifying
truth about the storms and the man who
controls them.

'The tension and excitement
never let up from the first page
to the last in this immensely
readable and thrilling
adventure story.'
Northern Echo

9781842706404 £4.99

When You Reach Me

REBECCA STEAD

Miranda's life is starting to unravel. Her best friend, Sal, gets punched by a kid on the street for what seems like no reason, and he shuts Miranda out of his life. Then the key Miranda's mum keeps hidden for emergencies is stolen, and a mysterious note arrives:

'I am coming to save your friend's life, and my own. I ask two favours. First, you must write me a letter.'

The notes keep coming, and whoever is leaving them knows things no one should know. Each message brings her closer to believing that only she can prevent a tragic death. Until the final note makes her think she's too late.

Winner of the John Newbery Medal 2010

Shortlisted for the Waterstone's Children's Book Prize

'Smart and mesmerising'
New York Times

9781849392129 £5.99

The
SNOW
MERCHANT

SAM GAYTON

Lettie Peppercorn lives in a house on stilts near the
wind-swept coast of Albion, with no one to talk to but
Periwinkle the pigeon. Her days are filled with floor-
sweeping, bed-making and soup-stirring. Her nights
are filled with dreams of her mother, who vanished
long ago. Nothing incredible has ever happened to
Lettie, until one winter's night.
The night the Snow Merchant comes.
He claims to be an alchemist – the greatest that ever
lived – and in a mahogany suitcase, he carries his
newest invention.
It is an invention that will change Lettie's life – and
the world – forever.
It is an invention called snow.

The Snow Merchant is a fantasy
filled with family secrets, magical
transformations and wild adventure.
Join Lettie on her journey to
uncover the true meaning of snow,
family and friendship.

Illustrated throughout by Tomislav Tomic

9781849393713 £12.99 Hardback